WICKED
IS THE
REAPER

CURSED CAPTORS

BOOK ONE

WICKED
IS THE
REAPER

NISHA J. TULI

To the girls who think the villain is kind of hot.

Chapter One

Twenty-three potential suitors stalked into the forest, each with the promise of a crown and a bride in their sights. They were an adequate, if uninspired, lot.

Standing at the tree line next to my sister, our mother and father flanked us on either side, our castle at our backs. They had forbidden us from entering the forest when we were children. The tales of the Reaper who haunted the trees pierced our dreams, leaving us lying awake and blinking in the dark. As we grew older, we still kept our distance, fearing the evil that rooted in its soil.

"Ellis looks so handsome today," my sister said in a wistful voice as she clung tightly to my arm. Two years my junior, Margaret would never share my fate. "You're so lucky, Rowan." My answering smile was tight as we both watched the man in question disappear into the dense trees.

For twenty-five years, I'd awaited this day. From the

moment I'd been old enough, I understood the Hunt would be the arbiter of my future. Today I'd be bound by fate, by circumstance, by the order of my birth, to the man I would marry and the man who would rule as king of Aetherus.

When the Fae had colonized our kingdom centuries ago, they'd left behind not only the blemish of their rule, but a decree—the Hunt would decide the betrothal of any royal first-born daughter. It was the way they had always done it in their own world, and we were to follow the same archaic rules that would see me handed over to a man without my say.

It had never been clear to me why the Fae cared at all, but I suspected it was to remind everyone who held the balance of our lives in their hands. Now, we'd wait here for hours as my stable of potential grooms hunted, killed, and delivered the largest stag to the feet of the king.

My father reached over and squeezed my hand, his smile gentle. "Don't worry, my love. Ellis will have this." Still clinging to my tight smile, I turned to my mother, who clasped my other hand in hers, her expression meant to be reassuring. We all bore the same dark hair, light brown skin, and deep brown eyes. My mother, Margaret, and I were near images of each other.

Everyone knew Ellis was the best hunter in Aetherus and though it wasn't a guarantee, today's odds swayed mostly in his favor. We'd been friends since we were children and had both understood this wasn't just my fate, but his as well. Ellis was handsome and kind and patient. I couldn't have asked for a better match. What we lacked in passion, we made up for with respect, friendship, and a mutual desire to do right by the people we'd rule.

Anyone in Aetherus was eligible to participate, but the resources and training needed were the privilege of only the wealthy. Despite the confidence in the Hunt's outcome, every eligible noble-born son in the kingdom had, nevertheless, arrived to throw in their lot. After all, their prize was a princess and a crown to go with it.

Even if there was an upset and someone else proved victorious, I knew these men. Had known them for years and none interested me either. Maybe some small part of me wished an unexpected suitor had shown up to try their luck, but I kept that errant thought to myself.

"How much longer?" I asked as the sun was setting, my feet tired from standing, my fingers numbing from the cold. I strained for the sounds that would signal anyone returning, praying this would be over soon. This entire spectacle was demeaning.

Behind us stood the whole of my father's court, quietly waiting. Casting a look over my shoulder, I caught their anxious glances. What did they have to be worried about? I was the one being handed off like a dog-eared book at the market.

With a frown, I turned away, my breath fogging in the air. As the hours wore on, the temperature dropped. It was nearing the end of autumn, the chill of winter's breath on the wind.

The leaves rustled, drawing my attention back to the trees. A man emerged with a dead stag draped across his shoulders. Hunched over from the weight, his steps were measured and steady. He crossed the tree line, stopped several feet from where we stood and dropped the stag on the ground.

He was a son of a lesser noble. Tyrion was his name, if memory served. He was a few years older, handsome in a classical if predictable way, but he was just window dressing. The stag was small by the standards of this forest, and he would pose no threat to my future.

A group of Fae-appointed overseers approached and began measuring, weighing, and cataloguing his kill for posterity. They would scrutinize everything to ensure we had followed their rules to the letter of the law.

When they were done, Tyrion stood and waited, his hands clasped behind his back as he cast surreptitious looks my way. More figures emerged from the trees, each one bearing their kill.

Every time another man appeared, my breath hitched as I anticipated a familiar head of dark brown hair. Ellis was the right choice for me. His family was influential, and he would make a good king. I didn't need that furious longing I'd read about in my favorite romance novels. Those were just stories. That wasn't real.

More suitors emerged from the trees, some of them looking decidedly less princely than they had this morning. Not every one of them would make it back alive. Stag hunting was dangerous, after all. That was the whole point of this barbaric tradition.

More and more hunters arrived, each dropping their bloody prize to be weighed and measured. The cloying smell of death and the forest's life taken hung in the air.

"Where is he?" Margaret asked, her brow furrowing. "I hope nothing happened to him."

I shared my sister's concern, worried Ellis had met with an accident. Even if he was the most skilled, that didn't make him immune to the spear of a stag's antler through his gut.

"He'll be here," my mother said, focusing on the forest. "Don't worry. Everything will be fine."

I nodded, doing my best to believe her when, finally, I spied a figure I recognized through the trees. My heart leapt in relief as Ellis trudged out of the forest with an enormous stag across his broad shoulders. He peered up through a fringe of dark lashes, throwing me a confident smile.

No, our relationship wasn't about lust or passion, but he was stable and loyal and would make a fine husband. That was better. That's what a queen needed.

He dropped his stag in the line and then straightened with a grin, his bright blue eyes sparkling. Blood covered his tunic, and there was a splash on his cheek, but otherwise he was whole. Looking down the row, it was obvious his kill was the largest, and I breathed a sigh of relief. Despite everything, he was still my first choice.

The overseers tabulated the numbers, assessing Ellis's stag. When they were done, they scurried to my father, all of them moving to the side to speak in soft whispers. Two hunters hadn't made it back, and now it was time to decide the victor.

My mother and I exchanged a glance before I looked over at Ellis and gave him a tentative wave.

When my father finished conferring, he strode over with

a beaming smile, his arms wide, ready to embrace his new son and welcome him to our family. "Ellis—"

"Not so fast," came a low, rumbling voice through the trees.

Every head turned to the sound as a figure emerged. It was enormous, wearing a long black cloak that brushed nearly to the ground, covered in thick shaggy fur. Its boots struck the earth with the cadence of a dirge as it approached, walking straight to where I stood with my family. Covered with a hood, its head was bent low with the weight of its enormous burden.

With a grunt, the figure heaved the biggest stag I'd ever seen off its shoulders and dropped the carcass at my feet with a resounding thud.

Chapter Two

I stared at the dead animal, trying to fit my thoughts together, but shock dissolved them like sugar spun thread.

"The Reaper," my mother whispered, her hand gripping mine so tight my fingers went numb. Margaret screamed, ducking behind me as my father stepped forward, shielding us both with his arm.

"What is the meaning of this?" he asked in his most commanding voice.

The figure then looked up. It wore a matte black mask in the shape of a leering skull, its row of menacing teeth flashing gold. It was the specter of death. A vision to make you believe in the possibility of all your worst fears.

We all knew the stories—nightmares charged with tales of the Reaper and what he did to those he dragged into the forest. The dead girls we'd found over the years. Their hearts ripped from their chests, their vacant eyes staring at the sky, their mouths open with the last screams they'd never utter.

"I'm competing for the hand of the *princess*," the Reaper said, his voice like rusty chains dragged over stone. He spat the word 'princess' like it was an embittered curse he'd found amongst a heap of garbage. I took a step back from the force of it, where I bumped into Margaret, who squeaked as I trod on her foot.

This monster wanted to marry me?

"You can't," my father said, drawing himself up.

The grotesque mask swung to me and then back to my father. The only thing visible was a pair of dark, glittering eyes, sharp as knife points. He tipped his head like a wolf scenting prey, the movement so feral it was as though the forest had born him straight from its roots. "Is it not the right of every citizen in Aetherus to compete in the Hunt, *Your Majesty?*"

My father's chin quivered, and his hands balled into fists. "Yes..." He stopped, searching for an answer that failed to materialize. "But you didn't enter this morning. You must enter."

"Actually," one overseer remarked, raising a bony finger. "That is merely a courtesy. It isn't part of the rules."

My father's nostrils flared, a muscle ticking in his jaw. He threw the overseer a murderous glare, and the man swallowed, perhaps realizing he'd just enjoyed his final moments on this plane.

The Reaper took a step closer, and a collective hush whipped around the clearing like autumn leaves kicked up on the wind. My father wasn't a small man, but the Reaper towered over him. "Record my stag," the Reaper said.

Huffing out deep, angry breaths, my father faced off

with the Reaper, his cheeks red, and his eyes wild. The overseer, who had spoken up, took a tentative step forward, bowing to the king who, after a moment, gave a strained nod.

My father had no choice, I realized. These were the rules of the Hunt. Failure to comply would bring down the wrath of the Fae and their wanton brutality.

The overseer dashed forward, stretching out his measuring tape as his helpers heaved the stag onto the scale. This was pointless, though. Anyone with eyes could see the Reaper's stag overshadowed the rest. I exchanged a look with Ellis. Held in a trance, he finally snapped and strode forward, his shoulders set with purpose.

He grabbed my arm and pulled me close, staring at the Reaper, whose grotesque mask seemed to grow more animalistic with each passing second. The demon's eyes flicked back and forth between us, and if I hadn't known any better, I'd swear they simmered with amusement.

I huddled closer to the man I was *supposed* to marry, suddenly wanting to be nowhere else but safe and cherished in his arms. This was where I belonged. Ellis pulled me tight, whispering reassurances in my ear.

Finished with their task, the overseers stood and faced the king.

"This...contestant's stag is the largest by several orders, Your Majesty. Unless there are any other claimants—" he paused, sucking in an audible breath "—the Reaper is the winner of the princess's hand."

A cry rose around the clearing as my entire future dissolved into a puff of ashes at my feet.

"No!" Ellis said, wrapping his arms around me. "No, I will not allow this."

My father studied us both, grim resignation in his expression.

"This monster cannot be the king!" Ellis cried, pointing at the Reaper. "You cannot mean to go through with this."

"I have no desire to be a king," the Reaper snarled through the mask, his voice darker than the pits of the underworld from which he came. "I'm taking her with me."

At that, my knees turned to jelly. It was one thing to be in the castle surrounded by my friends and family, but to be alone with him out in the forest? I'd be dead before the sun rose.

"You will not!" my father said, the words fused with molten rage. "She belongs here." He looked at his feet and then back up, rolling his shoulders before he grabbed an overseer by the collar of his robe. "Find a loophole in the rules. Something. Rowan is not going anywhere."

The overseers were already perusing the documents, conferring in hushed voices. But the same overseer who'd spoken earlier shook his head. "I'm sorry, Your Majesty. There is nothing preventing him from taking her. He has won, as per the rules of the Hunt."

"There must be something," my father hissed, towering over him. "Find something."

Ellis held me tighter, as though he could leash the trembling in my limbs.

"I'm sorry, Your Majesty," the overseer whispered, his voice quivering. "We can keep looking, but by the decree, the princess now belongs to the Reaper."

My mother covered her mouth while it opened in a soundless scream. "Gerald, you must do something," she sobbed. "Rowan cannot... she..." My mother trailed off as her eyes found the Reaper, who stood silently waiting for us all to come to terms with what I already understood. He knew his rights; I was his prize. No one could question that.

His gaze found me, those endless black eyes burning with the promise of my ruin, and I shivered. What did he plan to do with me?

My father groaned in frustration and ran a hand down his face. "There's nothing I can do." His words held the strain of a razor-fine edge.

He looked at me with a significance that traversed the space between us. All our hopes and dreams were gone. Everything we'd planned and wished for was over, dead and buried in the cold, hard ground. I had no choice. "I'm sorry, Rowan," he said with so much heartache, it wove into my soul, where I feared it would live forever. "This is never what I wanted for you. I should have taken precautions, but I never thought—"

Ellis pulled me closer, his arms like iron bands. "You can't mean to go through with this," he said, his voice cracking. "Your Majesty."

I shook my head and pulled his arm away. "I have to," I said softly. "If I don't, the Fae will come. I can't let that happen to any of you."

"Rowan," Ellis said, cupping my face in his hands. There was something eternal in his gaze. The buried promise of the future we would never have. "I'll come for you," he vowed. "I'll find some way to get you out of this bargain. I swear it."

I nodded, sure that was a promise he couldn't keep.

"While this is all very touching," the Reaper said, his tone mocking and bored, "we should get going before the sun sets any further."

The bastard didn't even care that he'd just destroyed my life.

He stepped forward, his heavy boots crunching through the leaves. Holding a rope, he grabbed both my wrists in one of his large, gloved hands and wrapped it around them.

"What are you doing?" I asked in shock. "I'm not an animal to be trussed up and dragged into the forest."

He secured my wrists with a knot. "That's where you're wrong, Princess."

"Rowan!" my mother screamed before the Reaper tugged me so hard I stumbled.

"It's okay, Mother. I'll be okay." I didn't believe that for one second, but what else could I say? Tears ran down her cheeks while my father clutched her. Margaret buried her face against my father's chest, sobbing.

Ellis moved in front of me as the Reaper yanked on my binding again. "I'll come for you," he vowed. "Be strong."

He turned to the Reaper. "If you hurt her, I'll cut out your heart myself and feed it to the palace dogs, and that would still be too noble an end for you."

The Reaper issued a derisive snort. "I'd like to see you try, lordling."

A vein in Ellis's forehead popped, and I swallowed,

trying to hold in my tears. I knew Ellis would try, but in my heart, I understood it was impossible.

"Come on, Princess," the Reaper said, his voice bearing a deadly purr that suggested if I didn't comply soon, he'd make us all sorry.

After stealing one last look at my stricken family, he tugged me again. I stumbled after, following him into the forest and into my nebulous future.

Chapter Three

We walked for what felt like hours, the sun sinking over the horizon and the stars glittering overhead. I'd never been this deep in the forest, and all I could see were miles of trees in every direction. Everything looked the same—a wall of green marking the boundaries of my prison.

Swerving confidently between the trees with the sinuous grace of a serpent, the monster to which I was tethered clearly knew exactly where he was going. His focus aimed at the path we trod, I stared at the wide expanse of his back, trying to obliterate him with the heat of my sizzling rage. But he continued unharmed, his long cloak fluttering in the air like the angel of death.

The fabric of my dress snagged on the brambles and branches, shredding the delicate silk into ribbons. I stumbled over my tired feet, but the Reaper never slowed his pace. I got the sense he wouldn't hesitate to drag me across the forest floor until my skin peeled off my bones if I fell. I harbored no illusions he'd entered the Hunt because he wanted to set up a home and make me his wife.

Ahead of us, an expansive range of rocky hills loomed, their tops dusted with browning greenery. They stretched for miles in either direction, forming a barrier symbolizing the divide between the future I'd been assured and the fate that now awaited.

As we drew closer, I noted a small opening that allowed us to pass through unheeded. I breathed a sigh of relief, knowing my delicate slippers would never survive the climb.

My stomach rumbled in hunger, and my throat crackled with thirst. It had been hours since we'd left the castle. I wondered what Margaret and my mother were doing right now. Was Ellis poring through texts, searching for a way to get me out of this? My father was likely ordering every one of his advisors to get me back.

But the decree was binding. The Fae had seen to that a long time ago. My only means of escape were death or the Reaper's release of his claim on my life. But this monster hadn't brought down the largest stag in the forest just to let me go.

No, I was his forever, no matter his reasons.

Just when I didn't think I could walk any farther, the trees parted, and a gentle hill rose across a small grassy plain. At the top stood a battered stone castle, looking like a single incisor left in a gaping, toothless smile.

I shook my head, unable to believe this sight, stunned to

find such a dwelling in the forest. Where had it come from? Who had once ruled here? The battlements were cracked and worn, the shattered windows like vacant eye sockets watching our approach.

Though it looked uninhabited, I understood with mounting dread, this was to be my new home.

The Reaper pulled me up the length of the well-trodden switchback to the massive wooden gate. He heaved one open with the heft of his shoulder, just enough that we could both slip inside.

Green moss grew over a small courtyard covered with cracked flagstones, many of them missing. Moonlight glinted off the smoothed, worn surfaces, and I could taste the eternal silence permeating the walls.

More moss muffled my footsteps as we crossed the space and entered another door at the far end. Pulling me inside a small room, The Reaper locked the entrance behind me. The only illumination came from a few small windows set high in the walls.

I surveyed the area, my eyes adjusting to the gloom. There was a beaten wooden table in the center, surrounded by three equally beaten chairs. Beyond that was a huge fireplace lining the wall, the hearth burning low. In the corner was a countertop and several cupboards that served as a kitchen, and in another corner was a large, neatly made bed.

As my gaze traveled across every angle, what I saw on the opposite wall made my blood run cold.

A cage.

The Reaper tugged on my rope, pulling me toward it,

and I yanked my hands back. "I'm not going in there!" I shouted, digging my heels into the stone floor. My delicate slippers offered no grip, and I slid like I was being dragged over warmed butter. I fought with every ounce of strength I could, but he didn't even seem to be trying.

"Please! I won't run. I promise." He pulled the rope so hard that I tripped and crashed into him. He was all muscle, as hard and unforgiving as iron. Before I landed on the ground, a large, gloved hand grabbed my upper arm and hauled me up to a standing position. "I'll stay put," I said again, and the Reaper let out a derisive snort that suggested he wasn't about to buy that.

With his enormous hand still wrapped around my arm, he shoved me through the door of the cage. My skirts tangling, I crashed into the far wall, my bound hands scraping the stone and my cheek grazing the surface. I winced at the sting when it broke my skin.

The cage door slammed with a metallic clang and then a click signaled the last remnants of my freedom, of my future, vaporizing into mist.

Wrapping my fingers around the bars, I shook them. "Let me out!" I shouted as loud as I could, but I might as well have been talking to a wall for all the attention the Reaper paid me.

After screaming for a minute, to no avail, I fell silent, deciding it was pointless. Instead, I watched the Reaper as he moved around the room, that hideous skull mask swinging from side to side.

Though he had an entire castle at his disposal, it seemed

he'd confined his life to only this room. He stoked the fire, the glow of orange flames offering more light and warming my numb fingers and toes.

Not taking my eyes off him, I watched as he pulled off his cloak and hung it on the wall. He then removed the thick overcoat underneath, revealing a black tunic. He appeared to be shaped like a human, his broad shoulders tapering to a narrow waist and thick, muscular thighs.

With his back facing me, he unbuckled the mask he wore, and I held my breath, prepared for the very worst. What horrors lurked beneath the mask of a creature known as the Reaper? After pulling it off, he shook out a head of wavy black hair that fell past his shoulders.

Curious, I stepped closer to my bars, watching while he removed his gloves and unbelted his weapons, dropping them all into a chest at the foot of his bed, which he then locked, stuffing the key in his pocket.

Then he stopped and stood stock still, as if feeling my eyes boring into him. He whipped around and I leapt back, again crashing into the wall behind me.

He was...normal? Almost normal, anyway, but for the line of dark markings that ran down the side of his face and throat and disappeared into his collar.

He smirked, apparently enjoying my distress, before he turned away and headed to the kitchen, where he opened the cupboards, retrieving plates, a loaf of bread, a hunk of cheese and thick slices of roasted beef. He deposited them on the table and then went to retrieve a pitcher of water, pouring two glasses.

It was then I noticed it.

He appeared normal, yes, but also not quite of this world. His skin bore a sheen, a near iridescence, his ears sweeping into delicate points. The way he moved like water flowing over river-worn stones marked him as anything *but* human.

"You're Fae," I whispered. "You're one of *them*." He looked over, the crescents of his dark eyes reflecting in the flickering fire, and grunted. "I don't understand. Why do you live out here?"

Ignoring my question, he continued his chores. While he worked, I examined my cage, noting the bare stone floor, absent of even a stool to sit on.

"You're going to keep me here like an animal?" I asked, my fury cresting. "Why do you have a *cage* in your home? The Reaper is a filthy *Fae*?" I spat the last word out with as much venom as I could muster, which finally secured his attention.

"Watch your mouth, Princess." His voice, no longer muffled by the mask, was still deep and rough, but less guttural.

"I will not! Why do you have a cage here? Who else have you locked up? Where are they?"

He stopped what he was doing and pinned me with a dark look. "You sure you really want the answer to that, Princess?"

I hesitated. Did I?

"Don't worry, they weren't all human," he said before he turned his back to me again. The proof of his statement was obvious from the state of the floor. It was filthy in here.

"You're really going to leave me in here like this? This is

disgusting." Tossing me a smirk, he pulled out a chair and sat down, pulling a plate of food toward him. "You won't be in there long."

While those words sounded promising on the surface, I knew not to trust them.

"Who are you?" I asked. "Why do they call you the Reaper?" The answer to that question wasn't one I was sure I wanted either, but I was here now and information might be the only weapon I had.

He shook his head, his lip curling in the corner. "I'm not the Reaper," he said, biting into a chunk of cheese. "The thing you humans call the Reaper is actually an ogre and lives somewhere deep in the woods."

I blinked. There were two monsters haunting the forest?

"Why does everyone call it the Reaper, then?"

The Fae-who-wasn't-the-Reaper arched a dark eyebrow. "Obviously, because it kills everything it sees. Not very clever, are you, Princess?"

I narrowed my gaze as he tore into a piece of bread and chewed slowly, savoring it along with the bitter tang of my distress.

"If you're not the Reaper, what do you want with me?" Another question and another answer I probably wouldn't like hung in the air like a rancid phantom.

"You're going to help me catch it," he said, casually taking a sip of water. My gaze followed the bob of his throat as he swallowed, and I licked my dry lips. His eyes darkening, he stared at me, his words collaring me around the throat with dread.

"How am *I* supposed to help you catch it?"

A grin stretched across his face. It marked him as something wild and feral, not entirely of this world. Something that refused to be tamed, no matter the shape of the whip.

"You're the bait, Princess.

Chapter Four

Sure, I had to have misheard, I frowned. "What?"

He didn't answer as he tore off another piece of bread and pointed it at me. "Hungry?"

"Don't change the subject. What do you mean I'm *bait*?" My voice had risen to a panicked octave.

He shrugged and popped the piece of bread in his mouth before he stood and approached the cage. I backed up, his imposing frame drawing closer. He pulled out a dagger from his belt, and I whimpered. "Get away from me!"

His shoulders dropped before he arched a dark eyebrow. "I was going to cut your restraints." He nodded toward my hands, where they were still bound. "Unless you prefer to stay that way."

Huffing out a breath, I slowly approached and held out my hands. He seized my wrist in one of his large palms, and I exhaled a pitched screech but didn't pull back. This close, I could get a better look at him.

The only Fae I'd ever seen were those who came to visit

once a year to ensure we were conforming to their unjust and numerous laws. But those Fae were very different. Their hair was light, usually so blonde it was white or silver. They had pale blue eyes, and their skin shimmered like starlight. They spoke in dulcet tones like they were trying to hypnotize us and moved through the castle as if they floated on gossamer clouds.

This Fae was entirely different with his dark olive skin and his black eyes. He didn't shimmer so much as he hummed with a sort of leashed energy. His face was pleasing if you looked past the fact he'd just stolen me from my home and was planning to feed me to an ogre. Those strange markings tattooed on his skin ran over high cheekbones and a sharp jaw covered in a thin layer of stubble. He had full lips, and dark angled eyebrows, and the honed form of a man used to fighting.

He sawed through my restraints, letting them fall free. I rubbed my sore wrists and backed away again.

"I'll let you out to eat something," he said. "But don't do anything stupid. You can't outrun me, and I know every corner of this forest intimately. Do you understand?"

The last thing I wanted was to share a meal with this beast, but my stomach growled in protest and it seemed my physical needs overruled my desires. Though I wasn't sure why he was feeding me, given he apparently wasn't keeping me here very long.

He was already unlocking the door, his eyes never leaving me. After opening it, he stood in the doorway. He was huge. At least a full head taller than me and nothing but tendons and muscle. It was obvious he was right when he said I couldn't outrun him. He moved like an apparition, all sinuous grace and lethal coiled energy.

"Your Highness," he said in a sarcastic tone, gesturing me to a chair at the table. I hesitated for a moment, but the simple fare looked delicious, and I was so thirsty. Brushing past him, I picked up a glass and drank the entire thing without pausing.

Dropping into my seat, I filled my plate with bread and cheese and meat and started eating with my hands. This was hardly the meal I was used to, but right now, it tasted like heaven.

The Fae sat down across from me and watched me eat.

"Rowan, was it?" he asked, picking up his glass and taking a sip of water.

"Why? Like you said, I won't be here long."

He snorted and placed the cup down. "Fair enough."

"What's your name?" I asked. "I'd like to know who I'll be cursing when the ogre is devouring me."

"Wicked," he said, and I burst into laughter and slapped my hand over my mouth. His eyebrows drew together, his intense gaze sparking.

"Is something funny, Princess?"

"That's not your real name. That's ridiculous."

His smile was cold as he leaned forward. "Well, it's the only one you're getting."

I rolled my eyes. "Fine," I said, stuffing bread in my mouth. "*Wicked*, it is." I made his name sound as ridiculous as it was, and his lip curled in a snarl.

"Watch it, Princess. You're alive at my mercy."

I leaned forward, baring my teeth. "You've already told

me I'm ogre food. What incentive is there for me to behave, *Wicked?* If I'm perfectly sweet and docile, will you change your mind and let me go home?"

He pressed his lips together, anger flaring across his expression. Oh good. I'd gotten under his skin. At least I'd accomplished that.

I sat back and folded my arms. "I didn't think so."

He glared while he pulled his plate closer and finished devouring his dinner. We ate in silence for several minutes, tossing dark, meaningful looks across the table. I noted my surroundings, including the only door and the high windows, pondering the best escape route. I had to get out of here, and fast.

"Why do you want to catch the ogre?" I asked casually. Maybe I could figure out his plans and how much longer I had to live.

"None of your business," he said, not taking his eyes off me as he chewed. He sat so still it was unnerving.

"I *do* think it's my business," I said in retort. "If you're planning to feed me to it, the least you can do is tell me why."

He leaned forward, and I mimicked his movement in expectation. "Get used to disappointment, Princess."

I growled low in my throat. "Asshole." He chuckled at that, and the sound was so human, so normal, it plucked my already stretched nerves.

Another minute passed before I tried again. Tracing a pattern into the wood of the table, I asked, "Then how about telling me *when* you plan to use me as bait for the reason that is none of my business?"

He didn't even humor me with a snort this time. Instead, I was rewarded with a resonant growl. "Keep this up and I'll make you sleep outside." His mouth stretched into a feral smile. "And what lives out there is much less friendly than I am."

Shivers climbed up my scalp at the menace in his expression.

"You just said you need me," I whispered, not sure who I was trying to convince. "You can't let anything happen to me until you get what you're after."

"I just need your blood, Princess. The rest of you is expendable."

I gaped at him, hoping he was just being dramatic, but there was only truth in his words. The room suddenly felt very small.

"You finished?" he asked, and I blinked in surprise, looking at my empty plate.

"Yes," I said softly, wondering how I was going to escape this nightmare. I thought of Ellis and Margaret and my parents. They must be beside themselves with worry. I thought of my soft, warm bed and my airy room in the castle. Of the feast I should have been enjoying after a betrothal to my oldest friend today.

Instead, I was here in this drafty, awful tomb with this cruel, wild Fae, about to become a snack for some monster I couldn't even imagine. The creak of the iron door of my cell roused my attention. Wicked held it open, his head tipped as he waited for me.

"In you go," he said.

"Can't I sleep there?" I pointed to the worn sofa in front

of the hearth. "I'll even take the floor. Please don't make me sleep in there." I willed as much docile subservience into my voice as I could. If he locked me inside, there would be no hope of escaping.

But if I thought Wicked had a compassionate bone in his body, I was sadly mistaken because he let out an evil chuckle that reminded me of the rattling bones scryers used to predict the future.

"Nice try, Princess. I'd like to get a good night's sleep without worrying about you trying to slit my throat and escaping." I bit my bottom lip. I hadn't even thought of the first part. Now I eyed the dagger hanging from his belt, mentally adding a new task to my list. He watched where my interest went, and it was obvious he knew exactly what I was thinking.

I bared my teeth in an attempt to look menacing, but he just rolled his eyes. "You can do as you're told, or I'll put you in there myself."

Wavering, I wished I could tear out a fistful of his hair and feed it to him. I couldn't fight him. I couldn't outrun him. My only hope was to find some way to outsmart him, but the cunning gleam in his eyes told me that wouldn't be easy to maneuver.

Slowly, I stood, my skirt clutched in my hands. My arsenal consisted of this wholly impractical dress, my cloak, and a pair of thin slippers. Basically, I had nothing.

With a withering glare, I glided into my cage and spun around to face him as he slammed the door in my face and locked it.

"Sweet dreams, Princess."

Chapter Five

I spent a miserable night on the cold, hard floor, huddled in the corner of my cell. The only warmth I had was from my cloak, which offered no insulation between me and the stone. Throughout the night, the fireplace burned lower and lower, the air growing so chilled I could see my breath in front of my face.

I called out to Wicked to stoke it with more logs, but either he ignored me or didn't hear, because he didn't stir from his bed on the far side of the room. I stared at the wide breadth of his back while he slept, hating him. Loathing him. He'd taken my entire life from me, and I would find some way to make him pay.

Plagued by murky dreams of the ogre and Wicked's perverse intentions, I drifted in and out of sleep. Eventually, I must have drifted off because the sounds of movement and the glare of sunlight woke me. Wicked stood in the kitchen, something sizzling on the cooktop. It smelled so intensely good; I sat up, wondering if he was planning to feed me again or if I was the one becoming the meal today.

At my movement, he turned to eye me, one of his dark brows already arched in disdain. "Hungry?" he asked, and tension loosened in my stomach.

Perhaps I had a bit longer yet to live.

I nodded, and he turned away, continuing what he was doing. While he finished cooking, setting the table and piling eggs and bacon onto a plate, I watched. The scent of coffee tickled my nose, and I scooted forward, pressing my face between the bars of my cage as I inhaled. After the miserable night on the floor, the reminder of these comforts felt like tiny jewel-encrusted lifelines.

When breakfast was ready, he approached my cage and unlocked it. The keen gleam in his eyes told me he wasn't about to let his guard down. With my gaze on my feet, I shuffled out of the cage, trying to look appropriately cowed. I had to trick him into underestimating me.

The derisive snort that followed in my wake suggested I hadn't fooled him for a moment. I tossed a piercing look over my shoulder that I hoped conveyed the vast depth of my acrimony. He ignored it and skirted around me to sit at the table, tucking into his food. My stomach growled, and I did the same after dropping in the chair across from him.

I took a bite of eggs and nearly moaned. It turned out this rogue Fae in the forest was a surprisingly skilled cook.

"Good?" he asked, catching my expression.

"It's fine, I guess. Not the absolute worst thing I've ever eaten," I said with a shrug. He smirked before he focused again on his plate. "So, what's on the schedule for today?"

When he looked up at me, I noted his eyes weren't black like I'd supposed last night. They were the deepest green, like the stinging needles of pine trees, sharp enough to slice through skin and draw blood. How appropriate. "You're going to stay here while I go scouting for a suitable location."

My stomach dropped. "A location for what?" I asked, my voice a whisper, knowing I should stop asking questions I didn't want answered.

"I've been tracking the ogre through the foothills of the Wasanan Mountains for the past three weeks. That will be a good place to set up tonight."

The rock in my stomach expanded, filling my limbs with dread. "Tonight?"

When Wicked had said I wouldn't be here long, he hadn't been exaggerating.

"Tonight," he repeated, his dark gaze meeting mine without flinching. If he felt any guilt about his plans, he was doing a very good job of hiding it.

Why would he feel any remorse, though? I was no one to him.

"Can't I come with you?" I asked. I didn't want to spend the entire day here alone in my prison, and if I could get some sense of my surroundings, maybe I could formulate an escape plan.

"No." His tone brooked no argument. "I don't need you getting in the way."

I pouted and tried to look pathetic, but that didn't move him at all. My appetite soured, I pushed the food around on my plate. He studied my motions like he was trying to read my thoughts, but said nothing as he rose and deposited his dirty plate in the sink. I did the same, standing up from the table and carrying it over to him.

He took it and looked down at me. I thought I saw a flicker of hesitation, but a moment later, he dumped the plate and then pointed to my cell.

"In you go."

"I need to use the bathroom," I said, trying to buy myself some time, and because I really needed to pee. He sighed, running a hand down his face.

"Right. Let's go." He opened the door and cocked his head for me to follow. I hesitated at the icy wisps of air that curled up my skirt and around my bared throat, making my skin dimple. "It's this or you go in the cage, Princess."

I nodded with my chin held high and followed him out into the cold, hating everything. When we were done, he ushered me inside and once again pointed to my cage.

I didn't bother protesting, already knowing it would be no use.

Wicked stomped through the room, collecting his weapons and shrugging into his thick coat. As I stood in my cell watching, he approached and closed the door, locking it, not meeting my eyes. He then donned the rest of his gear, including the long furred cloak and his gloves. He left the skull mask hanging on its hook.

"I'll be back in a few hours," he said, still not meeting my gaze. Tears burning the backs of my eyes, I nodded. This was really happening. He was going out to choose the ideal location to offer me up as a sacrifice for a monster. The edges of my vision smeared as I watched the future I'd envisioned shrivel away.

I wondered what Ellis was doing and if he'd found a way to get me out of this. Even if he did, I knew it would already be too late when he arrived. And that was supposing he could find this forlorn castle buried so deep in the woods.

Just as Wicked was about to leave, he stopped and looked at me before stomping over to the smoldering fire and adding another stack of logs, muttering to himself as if he was angry about doing so. He then gave a tip of his chin to no one and tossed me one more look before he swung open the door and slammed it behind him.

Chapter Six

After Wicked left, I paced in my cell, trying to hatch a plan. Maybe I could escape when he took me into the woods tonight. The problem was I was hours from home and getting there would mean having to find the pass that would allow me through the hills.

Even if I did, by the laws of Aetherus and the Fae, I belonged to him, and it would only be a matter of time before he found me and dragged me back here. I had no more rights than a sack of bruised apples.

The only way I could truly escape was to kill him. I needed a weapon. A dagger. A knife. Anything. I shook the bars of my cage, testing for weaknesses. But it was solidly built. If I screamed loud enough, would anyone hear me? Not likely. No one else lived in these woods and the villagers avoided the forest as much as they could because of the Reaper.

What would they think when they learned there were actually two monsters that called the forest home?

Frustrated, I let out a scream anyway just to relieve the pressure building in my chest. I screamed and screamed until my throat was raw and my voice gave out. It accomplished nothing, but it made me feel marginally better.

Sinking down into the corner of my cage, I wrapped my arms around my knees and waited for Wicked to return.

The sun was setting when the door slammed open, and he stepped inside. Snow dotted the furred shoulders of his cloak, and he shook it off, stomping his wet boots on the floor. I winced at the blast of cold air he brought with him. The fire he'd stoked had dimmed an hour ago, and the room had taken on a chill that left me shivering.

He rubbed his gloved hands, his breath fogging before he looked over to where I sat watching him. Without a word, he marched to the fireplace and added several more logs. Immediately, they caught fire, flaring brightly. It would take a while for the room to warm, and in the meantime, I tucked my frozen fingers into my armpits and glowered at my captor.

Wicked shucked off his overcoat and his gloves, hanging everything on the wall before locking his weapons in their trunk. Without looking at me, he headed for the kitchen, clearly intending to prepare supper. Would he feed me before he took me out into the woods? It hardly mattered. I had no appetite and couldn't have eaten a bite if I tried.

Before long, the aroma of cooking food filled the air. A large pot sat on the stove that Wicked tended to periodically. He didn't look at me the whole time, moving about his business. I sat in silence, simply observing.

When the stew was done, he portioned it into two

bowls. He also placed a bottle of wine on the table. Now that was an idea I could get behind. Maybe I could get drunk enough to dull my apprehension.

Finally, he approached my cage, unlocking the door and leaving it open before he stalked back to the table. Slowly, I rose and shuffled out, sitting in the seat across from him. The stew was a rich brown gravy floating with pieces of meat, carrots, peas, and potatoes. Any other time it would have smelled delicious, but right now, all it did was twist my stomach.

Ignoring the food, I snagged the bottle of wine, pulled out the loosened cork, and filled the glass in front of me to the top. Wicked watched me warily, saying nothing when I picked up the glass and chugged half of it back.

My mother would have been horrified. This wasn't the behavior of a princess. But I'd love to see how quickly she abandoned her so-called principles if *she* were kidnapped by a Fae and used as bait for an ogre.

Wicked remained quiet while I polished off the glass and then poured myself another. Outside, I noticed the snow falling more heavily, fat white flakes reflecting in the descending light.

Maybe he'd change his mind, but I doubted a little snow would stop him.

When we finished eating, he cleaned up the bowls and then turned to face me, grim resignation in his expression.

"It's time for us to go," he said.

I looked up at him with the most withering expression I could muster.

"How can you do this to me?" I whispered, my entire

body trembling. With rage. With fear. With the sick, crushing certainty, this was my last night on this earth. "I've never hurt anyone."

My venomous words landed where he was putting on his clothes, his shoulders stiffening. He paused for a breath and then resumed what he was doing, not looking at me.

"Get your things on," he said as he strapped his sword to his back and tugged on his gloves. With a nod, I stood and walked to my cage, where I picked up my cloak and wrapped it around my shoulders. My back straight, I faced him with my chin high. I'd at least go out with some dignity.

He opened the door and gestured me outside, where we exited to a sprinkle of gently falling snowflakes, the ground already covered in a thin layer of white. I rued the delicate slippers on my feet, wishing I had my boots.

When I'd stood at the edge of the forest with Margaret and my parents yesterday, I hadn't planned on going any farther than the tree line. We were supposed to wait for the victor of the Hunt and then return to the castle to settle into our rigid predestined roles. It was what I'd been prepared for.

Regardless, I vowed if I got out of this alive, I'd never leave my room again without thick socks and proper footwear.

Wicked slammed the door, causing me to jump and nearly stumble into the snow. My limbs were stiff and I couldn't get enough air. I'd never been so scared in my entire life. He brushed past me, his boots crunching.

"Come," he barked. Taking a deep breath, I picked up the

edge of my skirt and followed, tears flowing down my cheeks.

The air was mild, the wind still, which was a slight consolation. My cloak wasn't nearly warm enough for this weather, and my feet were already numb. Wicked stomped through the courtyard and into the forest, where our footsteps were muffled by the falling snow. In any other circumstance, it might have been beautiful.

He cast a look in my direction, his expression dispassionate, and then turned and started walking again. I did my best to keep up, but the ground grew increasingly slippery and my feet had turned into stumps of ice. I cried out when I lost my footing and landed on my ass so hard my neck cracked.

Wicked stopped and whirled around, fury in his dark eyes. With the glow of the moon and the falling snow and those strange markings on his face, he resembled an avenging god sent to deliver me to Hell. I cowered at the anger in his expression, no longer able to leash my fear.

Without a word, Wicked approached as I scrambled back. He bent down and then scooped me into his arms, cradling me against his body. I was too surprised to say anything as he once again started winding his way through the forest. I wanted to tell him to put me down, but it was a relief to be off my feet and he was so warm that I felt myself curling into his welcoming heat. I couldn't stop shaking.

He picked up his pace now that I wasn't holding him back and was flying through the trees at a speed that was dizzying. My arms circled around his neck, and I closed my eyes while my vision spun. Eventually, I chanced a look up at him. He stared straight ahead as though I wasn't there. He seemed to be holding his breath, his chest barely moving.

While he continued running, I buried my cold face in the curve of his throat. Gods, he was so warm. Right now, I didn't care that he'd brought me here to kill me. I was so frigid and miserable I would've snuggled up to the devil himself if he'd offered me a blanket.

We continued through the trees for a while longer before Wicked finally came to a halt, the forest so silent it seemed as if it, too, felt the weight of the crime about to unfold. Wicked set me on my feet and then dragged me to the center of a small clearing. Rocks and boulders surrounded us on all sides, blocking off my view and reminding me of the boundaries of my existence.

I was trapped here, and I was going to die.

Lying in the center of the clearing was a set of chains and manacles anchored into the ground. My mouth opened in horror, realizing this was what he'd been doing out here today. He didn't meet my eyes as he fell to his knees and secured them around my ankles and wrists. I said nothing while he worked, simply staring at him, wondering what kind of monster would do this to anyone.

Tears slipped down my cheeks, turning into burning rivers of ice in the cold air. Once he finished chaining me to the earth, Wicked stood and surveyed our surroundings.

"Are you really going to leave me out here?" I asked, forging steel into my voice. "I knew the Fae were terrible, but I didn't know you had absolutely no conscience."

He pinned me with a cold look. "Don't lump me in with the Fae."

I snorted out a hysterical laugh. "Are you kidding me? You're the worst of the lot! You stole me from my family! From the man I was supposed to marry! You ruined my entire life to use as bait for a monster. And you won't even tell me why!"

Wicked curled his lip, his dark eyes flashing, but said nothing in response to my outburst.

"I'll be hiding in the trees," were the only words he uttered before he stalked away.

"Fuck you!" I shouted at his back, relishing the words I was normally forbidden to utter. It felt good to let go of the metaphorical chains that once bound me, even if I'd now been snared by physical ones. It was the only comfort I had left. "You bastard! Come back and face what you're doing to me! You coward! You asshole!" I yanked on the chains, the iron manacles biting into my skin.

Once his dark form disappeared into the forest, panic twisted in my nerves. He said he'd be in the trees, but I felt completely alone. I listened to the noises of my surroundings, interrupted by the clicks of my teeth chattering. The snow continued to fall, covering me, soaking into my hair and clothing.

"Please don't do this," I pleaded to the darkened night. "I'll help you find another way. Anything you want, it's yours."

If Wicked could hear me, he gave no sign as I begged and pleaded for my life. When my voice gave out, I finally caved into silence. I'd lost all sense of time, but I was getting colder by the moment. I couldn't feel my toes or my fingers. The least this bastard could have done was ensure I didn't freeze to death before the ogre came for me.

Snow continued to fall until everything was coated in white. My eyelashes stuck together when I blinked, and the cold air made my lungs ache. Eventually, I sank to my knees, tired, exhausted, and no longer able to keep myself up. Instead of pleading for my life, I now pleaded silently for the ogre to end this misery.

A rustling in the leaves drew my attention, but the darkness prevented me from seeing anything beyond the clearing. My eyes drifted shut, and I collapsed to the ground, sliding in and out of consciousness.

Then I heard a snarl right next to my ear, but I was too cold and too tired to be afraid anymore. I welcomed the end.

But then I felt it. The soothing warmth of the fires of hell wrapping around me, bundling me into a cocoon of relief. As I let out a pitiful whimper, something lifted me into the air before I completely drifted away.

Chapter Seven

My face was pressed to a soft surface that smelled like the forest. Like soil after a rainstorm and the kiss of a warm spring breeze. I buried my nose deeper, savoring the silkiness against my cheek and the scent filling my lungs. Something heavy lay on top of me, and I groaned when I moved, my fingers and toes protesting. My muscles were sore and achy, and my head was throbbing.

Was this what awaited in the afterlife?

Finally, I peeled my eyes open, surprised to find myself in Wicked's small room. I was in the corner, lying on his bed with a mound of soft blankets covering me. My cage stood open across the room, and I squeezed my eyes closed, wanting to forget its presence. A shadow fell over me, and I looked up to find Wicked, eyebrows drawn together, a wooden spoon held in one hand.

He dropped into a crouch, bringing him to eye level.

"How are you?" he asked, his voice soft. I blinked, trying

to orient myself. He'd left me in the forest to die, and now this asshole was asking how I was?

"How do you think I'm doing? Why am I here?"

He had the grace to look abashed, his gaze dropping to the ground and the tips of his delicately pointed ears turning red.

"You passed out from the cold. Near onset of hypothermia, I think." Despite the moment of contrition, his voice was aloof as he rose and returned to the stove. Smells of warm, hearty food filled the room, and my stomach grumbled in response. He heard it and looked at me, something inscrutable in his expression.

"Dinner is almost ready," he said. "You can get changed."

"Dinner? How long have I been asleep?"

"Two days."

He turned away, resuming his task. It was then I noticed a large bag sitting next to the bed stuffed full of clothing. I sat up, noting the pair of winter boots next to it. *My* boots. Throwing off the covers, I dug into the bag and cried out with joy. These were *my* clothes. Warm tunics and thick calf-skin leggings. Wool dresses and flannel nightgowns. My heaviest cloak and fur overcoat.

I caught Wicked staring at me as I touched each object like it was a gift from the skies. "Where did these come from?" I asked, pulling out a pair of black fleece-lined leggings and my warmest tunic. A pile of wool socks at the bottom almost had me shouting in triumph.

"I went to the castle to get them for you. Your mother packed them."

My eyes narrowed with suspicion. "You went to the castle?" He nodded, laying out plates and cups on the table.

"Why?"

A casual shrug was his response. "You needed more clothing. I realized that the other night." I frowned at him, wondering what he was up to now.

"How's my mother?" I asked. "Did you see my father? My sister?"

A shadow passed over his expression. "Your mother and sister were well enough. Your father wasn't happy to see me."

I snorted at that. "Yes, well, you did steal his eldest daughter, and he doesn't even know the half of what you plan to do with me. He probably figured you just wanted to have your way with me."

Wicked's eyes flashed. "I stopped a servant outside and told them to send your mother out. She asked about you, and I told her you were fine."

I laughed again, the sound doused in acid. "Yes, I'm great. Just a little monster bait, that's all. It's the idyllic marriage I always hoped for."

He said nothing as he returned to the kitchen, chopping tomatoes and sliding them into a bowl.

"What happened? Why am I currently not digesting in the Reaper's stomach?"

Wicked said nothing for so long I thought he wouldn't answer before he finally replied, "It didn't come."

"Oh," I said, an amorphous hope taking shape in my chest. "I guess it's not interested in me, then. You should probably just let me go. No hard feelings, okay?" I planted my feet on the ground and prepared to stand.

Wicked turned around, a platter covered in food suspended in his hands. He threw me a dark look before he placed it on the table. "We'll try again."

I sucked in a breath. "Right. Of course." It couldn't be that easy. I'd still have to find a way to kill him. He'd been foolish enough to bring me proper clothing and boots, which offered an advantage I hadn't had yesterday. Maybe if I remained patient, I could lull him into complacency. Learn to play the good little prisoner until the right moment for escape presented itself.

The fire roared on the far side of the room, but the temperature was dropping with the onset of evening, and I shivered in my dress. The skirt had been shredded, and it was effectively ruined.

"I want to get changed," I said, holding up the clothing I'd selected.

"Then change," he said, staring at me, folding his thick arms as he leaned against the counter, one ankle crossed over the other.

"Not with you watching me," I hissed. He huffed out a laugh, a wicked gleam in his eye.

"Shy, Princess?"

"No," I bit back. "But I'm not giving *you* a show. Maybe you *do* still want to use me for other lurid reasons."

His expression darkened. "I would never do that," he snarled.

"No, you'd just leave me out in the forest alone in the cold to die! But I guess you're not so bad because you'd draw the line at raping a woman! Do you want a knighthood for that?"

He pressed his mouth together, his lips turning white and fury flashing in his evergreen eyes. Oh my, I'd pissed him off. Gods, that felt better than it really should.

"Fine, if you're so damn noble, turn around and stay that way until I say so. Close your eyes too." He didn't argue, facing the countertop and bracing his hands against it, his head dropping between his shoulders.

When I was satisfied he'd remain in that position, I changed as quickly as I could, keeping myself covered with the blanket and hoping he would keep his eyes where I wanted them.

An awkward silence settled over the room while I stripped out of my ruined dress and slid on my warm clothing. I practically moaned at the lush fabric when it pressed against my skin. After putting on two pairs of socks, I found my house slippers in the bag and stepped into them.

When I was fully covered, I said, "Okay, I'm done."

He looked over his shoulder, scanning me from head to toe. His dark gaze was so intense, something unfamiliar tugged low in my stomach in response.

"Don't expect a thank you for treating me with a modicum of decency," I snapped, wanting to dispel the strange tension he'd just fired in my chest.

"I'm not." His voice was low and rough and that, too, affected me in a way I didn't care to examine.

I cleared my throat and ran my fingers through my dark waves, trying to smooth out the tangles. I dug into the bag again and was delighted to find my brush. Sitting at the table, I ran it through my hair while Wicked finished preparing our meal. He set down the rest of the food: a fresh salad of greens and tomatoes, a platter with poached fish, and a bowl of roasted potatoes swimming in gravy.

"Where do you get all this from?" I asked.

"From the village," he said, surprising me with the answer. Surely, I'd have heard about someone like him wandering the marketplace before. He wouldn't blend in anywhere.

"Do you go there often?" I scooped up a mound of potatoes and dumped them on my plate, along with a big piece of fish. I was starving.

He shrugged and sat in his seat, and I resisted the urge to throttle him for this string of evasive answers. "Right," I said. "Fine."

He looked up at me, a bright spark in his expression before he filled his plate and started eating. We "enjoyed" another silent meal, the air weighted with a charge I didn't understand. When we were nearly done, I asked, "So what's the plan? Am I going into the woods again tonight? Surely you want to get my murder over with?"

Wicked's eyes darkened as he peered up at me through a fringe of thick black lashes. It was frustrating to notice how beautiful he was. Objectively speaking, of course. He was nothing like Ellis or the other men who'd tried to vie for my hand the day of the Hunt. Though many had been handsome and pleasing, Wicked seemed to exist outside such simple and benign words. There was something wild and savage in the hard lines of his face and the dips and curves of his lean body. His eyes gleamed with something raw and ancient, like a beast that had been forgotten at the edge of the world.

It was hard not to notice, even if he was a complete and utter jackass.

"No," he said. "Not tonight. Tonight you rest. I'll have to scout for another location. It'll take me a few days."

The tension in my shoulders eased a bit at that. A few days. That gave me some time to figure out a plan to get out of here.

As Wicked continued eating, I took stock of my surroundings. He kept his weapons locked away in a trunk at the foot of his bed whenever he was home, except for the dagger he kept on his belt. The kitchen knives were blunted things that, in theory, weren't dangerous, but used correctly could do some damage.

I'd need to do more than just hurt him, though.

To earn my freedom, he had to die.

Chapter Eight

After supper was complete, I stretched into a yawn. My time in the forest had left me exhausted, and I was ready to sleep for another few days. I eyed my cage morosely, imagining a night on the cold, hard ground. Wicked caught my stare and bit his bottom lip, indecision in his gaze.

"You can sleep in the bed," he said, finally.

I narrowed my eyes. "Where will you sleep?"

"On the sofa," he said. It looked too small to accommodate his large frame, but I was hardly worried about that.

"Fine." I stood and headed toward the bed when Wicked intercepted me.

Though he didn't lay a hand on me, he stood so close I had to crane my neck to look into his face. Warmth siphoned off him in waves, and I remembered the way he'd carried me in the woods. How good it had felt to press myself up against that wall of heated muscle. I shook my head. My brain was addled from all this stress. The only reason I'd needed his warmth was because he had put me in that situation in the first place.

"I'm trusting you not to do anything stupid," he said, his voice practically a growl. He leaned closer, and I looked away, my gaze finding the door and the only exit from my prison. Strong fingers found my chin before he directed my face back to him.

"Rowan," he said, and I blinked, surprised to hear my name on his lips and trying not to notice the illicit way my heartbeat kicked up when he growled it like that. Like he intended to break me apart and see what I was made of. "I mean it. You'll get lost out there and it's dangerous. You can't run from me. I'm stronger and faster, and I can scent your trail for miles. There's nowhere you can go."

His face was so close to mine, I could feel the whisper of his breath on my lips. He smelled like his bedsheets. Like the forest and fresh, earthy things. In the pit of my stomach, I felt a conflicted shiver as my mouth parted.

For a moment, we hung suspended in a trance, our gazes warring with a churning sea of unspoken thoughts.

What was happening to me?

"Okay," I lied, finally finding my voice somewhere at my feet. I'd use any opportunity I could to get out of here. No matter what he said, I'd have to take my chances in the forest.

He stared at me for another moment and then nodded, before heading to the kitchen to clean up after our supper.

I didn't offer to help. He'd stolen me from my family and my life to use as bait and he could do the fucking dishes himself. I kicked off my slippers and, without

another word, slid under the warm covers and promptly
fell asleep.

IT WAS FULLY dark outside when I awoke, the fire burning low
in the hearth. The room was warm and cozy, and I snuggled
deeper into the covers when the soft sounds of sleep drew
my attention. Wicked sat on the floor with his back against
the bed and his head tipped to the side. I rolled my eyes. I
guess he hadn't trusted me enough to remain on the sofa on
the other side of the room.

He breathed heavily, his shoulders moving up and down
in a rhythmic pattern. If he believed that would stop me, he
wasn't as smart as he thought.

Slowly, I eased out of the bed, placing my socked feet on
the cold ground. When I glanced at Wicked, I sucked in a
breath. His top half was bare, that strange line of tattoos
continuing down his throat and over his smooth chest,
down his ribs and along the side of his chiseled stomach. He
looked like he'd been carved from stone, and I took a
moment to admire the curve of his broad shoulders and
what had to be the most exquisite collarbone I'd ever seen.
My eyes trained on the dark line of hair that ran under his
navel and disappeared into his waistband, before my cheeks
flushed with heat.

He was a monster, but...wow.

Finally, I gathered my wits and scooted over to where
my boots sat next to the bed. I quickly laced them on,
keeping one eye trained on Wicked, not allowing my gaze to

wander south of his chin, but I wasn't sure that was any better. Why had the gods seen fit to turn this beast into the perfect specimen of male beauty?

I shook my head and forced myself to focus.

He shouldn't have trusted me, not for a moment.

I noticed the dagger he always wore was tightly gripped in his large hand. Fuck. There was no way I could get it. I quietly shuffled to his weapons trunk and found it securely locked. I knew he kept the key in his pocket, but there was no chance I could dig into it without rousing him. And then the idea of putting my hand in his pants caused my cheeks to flush again.

Focus, Rowan.

As I noted earlier, the utensils in the kitchen wouldn't do me much good either. He'd already locked away anything sharper than a butter knife. I could try sticking one in his eye, but that wouldn't kill him, just make him really angry. I didn't need to experience his Fae strength to know he could overpower me in a heartbeat.

Fuck it. I'd just run. If I could make it back to the castle, maybe I could seek safety behind those walls while I figured something out. My father couldn't go against the decree, but maybe we could stall for time.

With another glance at Wicked, I put on my cloak and fastened it before tugging on my mittens. I took a deep breath to steady my pounding heart and then crept for the door on silent feet and eased it open. Thankfully, there was no wind tonight, making that one less thing to worry about.

Keeping my eyes on him, I opened it a little wider until I could slip through. He continued sleeping, his chest rising and falling, the gleam of the fire glinting off his smooth tanned skin. I slipped out the door and eased it closed.

After it was shut, I waited, holding my breath. Had I really succeeded?

When I didn't hear any movements on the other side, I let out a relieved breath and then turned and ran for my life.

Chapter Nine

The moon was high, offering me plenty of light as I made my way across the courtyard and through the gates of the ruined castle. The forest became a blur as I raced through the trees, heading toward my home.

My hair whipped across my face, my cloak billowing as it caught on the branches of the bushes and trees. I considered discarding it to speed my flight, but it was too cold. If I had to hide somewhere when morning came, I'd need it. My breath fogged in the air in hot gusts, and I tried not to think about what might be lurking in the shadows as I ran.

Casting a look behind me, I tried to discern if I was being followed. Hopefully Wicked wouldn't awake for hours, and by then I'd be long gone. But my stomach sank when I realized a dark blur was racing through the trees, and it was gaining on me quickly.

"Shit," I muttered under my breath when suddenly the ground disappeared under me, and I pitched forward with a scream. I was rolling down the side of a steep incline, tumbling end over end, branches and brush scratching and scraping at my skin. A sharp pain dragged along my shoulder, and I screamed again as I spun in a blur.

Finally, I came to a jarring stop at the bottom of a steep ravine. I groaned, my body aching and my shoulder on fire. I couldn't tell if I'd broken any bones, but I hurt everywhere.

Above me came the soft rustle of something moving through the trees. The moonlight illuminated a familiar form racing toward me. Wicked was still only half dressed as he bounded down the hillside, his expression so wild with anger it seemed to gather speed and roll over the ground to where it found me at rock bottom.

I tumbled over and pushed myself up, my body protesting and blood gushing where my shoulder ached, its warmth dripping down my arm and side. I must have hit something on my way down. With a heave, I stood up and limped along the floor of the ravine. There was no way I could outrun him, especially not like this, but I couldn't just lie there and wait.

It took less than a handful of seconds before I heard a grunt and felt his arms wrap around my thighs before he hauled me up over his shoulder. I cried out in protest as my arm throbbed painfully. Wicked paid me no mind as he spun and began making his rapid way back up the side of the mountain. It was then I realized how much he'd held himself back earlier as he ran so fast I felt the resistance of the wind on the backs of my legs.

Hanging off his shoulder, the world spun in my vision, and I gripped the waist of his pants to anchor myself, worried he'd drop me. Before I knew it, I recognized the switchback that led to his castle and then the grounds of the courtyard. I heard the door slam open and then close before he dropped me onto the bed in an unceremonious heap.

I moaned in pain, blood gushing from my wound. Wicked was tugging at my cloak, his skin reflecting a sheen of sweat and his pallid face a mask of fury. "You foolish, foolish princess," he growled. "I told you that you wouldn't get away."

"Fuck you," I managed weakly while he pulled off my cloak. Blood covered the entire side of my tunic.

"What did you do?" he hissed before he rose and moved from the bed. I heard him shuffling around in the kitchen before he returned a moment later. "I'm going to roll you over."

His hands were more gentle than I would have expected, but the movement sent a sharp pain through my back that caused me to gasp. "Sorry," he said softly. I heard the rip of fabric when he tore away my blood-soaked tunic and then the gentle touch of a warm wet cloth as he cleaned the wound. While he tended to my injury with soft touches and the occasional grunt of irritation, I lay there, not moving. I sensed he wanted to launch into a lecture about my recklessness, but was saving it for later. Something to look forward to, then.

He pulled out a white roll of bandage and placed it across my shoulder, his hands sliding under my arm as he wrapped it around me securely. I tried not to think about how close his fingers were to my naked breast and how nice they felt on my skin. When he was done, he placed a soft hand on the center of my back and leaned forward to examine his work. A ripple traveled over my skin as his thumb swept back and forth in a soft caress. "I think it'll be okay," he said. "It was a clean cut, even if it was deep. It'll take a little while to heal. I'll see if I can get some stronger ointment from the village tomorrow."

His gaze met mine, firelight reflecting off his dark eyes. I wouldn't apologize for trying to escape, but there was something so tortured in his expression, a small part of me almost felt guilty for running.

"Thank you," I said, meaning it. He could have left me lying at the bottom of the ravine as a sacrifice for the ogre. A part of me wondered why he hadn't.

"You don't have to thank me," he said, his tone gruff as he stood up and went back to the kitchen. My eyes drifted shut as I gritted my teeth against the sharp pain lancing through my back. A few moments later, he returned with a steaming mug. His hand resting on the small of my back again, he held it to my mouth. "Drink some of this. It'll dampen the pain and help you sleep."

I lifted my head, and he gently tipped the mug. The liquid was warm and soothed my throat, tasting of honey, lemon and lavender. I moaned in appreciation as the effects kicked in almost immediately. He made me drink some more, and the pain slowly ebbed, my eyelids growing heavier.

Just before I fell asleep, I felt the brush of his fingers sweeping up my spine and then against my forehead before he tucked a lock of my hair behind my ear.

"What are you doing to me, Rowan?" he asked softly before I drifted into sleep.

Chapter Ten

I awoke to the soft sounds of Wicked's breathing, his face just inches from mine. He lay on the bed, his top half still bared and his hands folded over his stomach. I didn't move a muscle, only scanning him while I studied the strange tattoos that ran down the side of his face and torso, wondering what they meant.

A moment later, the back of my neck prickled. I looked up to find him watching me, his gaze thoughtful and brimming with concern. I became immediately aware we were both half naked, though I was on my stomach. It occurred to me he must have seen my bared chest while he was tending to me, and I frowned. But his touches had only been tender and caring last night.

He'd said he wasn't that kind of monster, and I was inclined to believe him on that, at least.

"I hope it's okay. I wanted to keep an eye on you, and I guess I dozed off before I could move to the sofa," he said. It took me a moment to realize he was apologizing for falling asleep in the bed. I moved my head, my hair rustling against the mattress.

"It's fine."

He relaxed visibly at that. Neither of us moved while we lay there in silence, our gazes meeting and then pulling away as though neither of us could quite figure out what to do with ourselves. Finally, he sat up, and I did my best not to notice the flex and pull of the muscles in his back and his arms while he leaned over to stretch and then rubbed his hands down his face.

"How are you feeling?" he finally asked. I shifted, testing my shoulder, and winced at the stab of pain.

"Okay. A little sore."

"Hungry?" he asked, looking over at me, and I quickly averted my gaze lest he catch me staring. "I'll make you some more tonic for the pain, too."

"Sure, thank you," I replied before he scooted off the end of the bed and padded over to the kitchen. He got to work as I closed my eyes, curiously soothed by the now familiar sounds of him cooking.

For the next few days, Wicked tended to me, changing my bandages regularly and bringing me food and water and more pain tonic. While I healed, I drifted in and out of sleep until I could finally sit up and move my arm again. The wound was still healing, but I'd improved considerably.

Wicked didn't leave the entire time, save once, to pick up the healing ointment he'd promised, tending to me with all the attention of a doting nurse. Why was he bothering? Did he need his sacrificial lamb in tiptop shape the next time he abandoned me in the forest?

Still, I couldn't fault him for the careful way he tended to me, even if it was technically his fault I'd been hurt in the first place.

It was about a week later before I could move around and take care of myself again. I'd been sleeping in his bed every night, but now that I was feeling better, the question hung between us.

"We can keep sharing the bed," he said, not meeting my eye as he cleaned up the dishes after supper. "If you want."

The discomfort of sleeping in my cell overriding any of my reservations, I nodded. Wicked had been the perfect gentleman already, clearly going out of his way to stay on his side of the bed. If he'd wanted to try something, he'd already had ample opportunities.

"I'll have to chain you to it, though. I can't have you running off again."

I folded my arms. "Absolutely not."

He turned to face me, leaning against the counter and crossing one ankle over the other, hands braced against the edge. "Then you can sleep in your cell." The look on his face brooked no argument, and I knew I wouldn't win this one.

My nostrils flared in indignation. "Fine."

"Glad you can see reason, Princess," he said in the most condescending voice possible. I wrapped my hand around my butter knife, strategizing on where I could shove it so it would do the most damage. He caught the movement and then smirked.

"Don't bother. I'm a hundred times stronger than you could ever hope to be, Princess." He rewarded my glower with a smug smile before he turned his back on me, confident I posed absolutely no threat.

Later, when I crawled into the bed at my place against the wall, he did what he'd promised, digging out one of those manacles he'd used on me earlier, securing it to my ankle and then the bed. It left me free to move, but fuck if it wasn't demeaning. He then gave me a pointed look and stuffed the key deep into his pocket, as if to remind me there was no way I was getting to it.

"Don't think I'd hesitate to reach in your pants for the key if the opportunity arose," I said, not entirely sure if it was a joke. Instead of the reaction I'd expected—a roll of his eyes or a glare—his mouth fell open and then snapped shut and...gods, was he blushing?

Suddenly I didn't know where to look as my own face heated. He cleared his throat before he looked away, pretending to busy himself with his boots as he pulled them off.

He turned down the lamps, leaving only the glow of the hearth, and lay down next to me. As the mattress dipped, I felt the tangible weight of his presence like a flashing beacon. The silence we normally shared had shifted, stretching between us with a tension molded from what felt like a thousand thoughts neither of us wanted to acknowledge.

Trying to scatter the heaviness in my chest, I rolled to my side, my back facing him. It did nothing to quell the uncomfortable tightness that pulled low in my stomach.

"Good night," he said softly, but I didn't answer.

A FEW DAYS LATER, Wicked announced, "I'm going to do some scouting today."

The reality of my situation came crashing to a shuddering halt. We'd been enjoying an easy sort of truce while I'd recovered from my fall. I'd almost forgotten why I was here and why he'd stolen me from my home. Maybe some part of me had thought he'd changed his mind, but clearly I was wrong. Why had he bothered to take care of me at all?

"Can I come?" I asked, and he pinned me with a dark look.

"You've got to be kidding me, Princess."

I shrugged. "It was worth a try."

There was a small tug at the corner of his mouth, but he said nothing while he continued dressing. When he was done, he'd erased all traces of humor before he pointed me back to my cage.

This time, he did me the courtesy of cleaning it up and providing some blankets and pillows, along with food and water and even a few books to pass the time. It was still a cage, but it was a little more pleasant. A small part of me could hardly blame him for locking me up. I wouldn't trust myself either, and I was far from finished with my escape attempts. As far as I was concerned, that dagger still had his name on it.

After he locked it, he stared down at me for a moment and I stared back, my expression defiant, willing him to feel the shame of what he was doing. There was a flicker in his gaze. A hairline crack in his stony facade that I planned to manipulate to my advantage. Then he grunted and spun away before storming to the door and slamming it so hard it shook the walls.

His footsteps crunched in the snow, fading away before I sat back and waited.

Chapter Eleven

T he next week continued in the same vein as I continued to recover. When he was home, Wicked never let me out of his sight and never let his guard down.

Every day, he'd go out for hours and leave me locked up, returning as the sun was setting to make us dinner. Our conversation flowed surprisingly easily while he asked me questions about my family and my life. There was something calming about being away from the castle and all my former obligations. The role of heir was never one I particularly relished.

Wicked seemed to love listening to the stories of me and Margaret getting into all sorts of trouble and appeared genuinely interested in everything I had to say. I couldn't figure him out and as the time wore on, I sensed us both easing into an unfamiliar place where our walls were thinning at the seams.

Though I was enjoying myself, maybe even a little too

much, the idea that I might charm him into releasing me was never far from my mind. Once in a while, I'd catch a genuine smile when I recounted some silly tale from my childhood. It transformed his entire face, rendering even those fearsome tattoos into something far more innocent.

I tried to fish for information about him, both because I was genuinely curious, but also because I desperately wanted to know why he wanted to capture the ogre and why I was being made his unwilling sacrifice.

Every time I'd steer the conversation toward him, he'd clam up and then order me to bed, the conversation done for the night. He still chained me to it, though I suspected he did so with increasing reluctance.

He always slept without his tunic, maintaining a respectful distance that did nothing to subdue the heaviness that settled in the room every night. The sight and scent of his bare skin was a complete distraction and more than once I found myself wondering what it would be like to touch him, to smooth my hands over the swell of his shoulders or the lines of his chest. To drag my fingers down the planes of his stomach and explore...lower. I didn't understand these indecent thoughts I was having more and more often. My emotions were turning into a jumble of warring desires threatening to tow me under.

It was about three weeks after I'd tried to run when I awoke one morning with my face buried into a cocoon of velvet that smelled of forests and the rain. Groaning in approval, I snuggled closer into the column of warmth. Then I cracked open my eyes, suddenly realizing what I was wrapped around. I looked up, hoping against hope he was still asleep and I could disentangle myself with no one the wiser.

However, a pair of curious pine green eyes regarded me. No such luck.

"Comfy?" he asked, a dark eyebrow arching. Frozen, I didn't move, realizing that my arm and leg were both thrown across him.

"What did you do?" I accused, not really wanting to move. He was so warm and solid, and this felt better than I wanted to admit.

"This is my side of the bed, Princess. You're the one who did something." I looked behind me and sure enough, it had been me who'd clearly rolled over and was now lying practically on top of him.

"Shut up," I said as I finally forced myself away, sitting up and scooting back until I hit the wall. Wicked tossed me a smirk before he rose from the bed. He quickly reached for his tunic and covered himself, but our gazes met, knowing we'd both just noticed the clear outline that stretched in the front of his breeches.

"It's morning," he stammered then, his face turning red. Oh, this was too good. "And your thigh was right where..." His nostrils flared and he tossed me a glare. "Shut up." Then he turned and stomped away, not looking at me before he donned his tunic and washed his face in the basin in the corner.

When he unlocked my ankle, I continued grinning while he refused to meet my eyes. I willed myself not to check that rather interesting part of his anatomy again, sure I wouldn't be able to keep the same blush off my face.

Wicked started on breakfast, as always. It amazed me how he fed me and cleaned up every day without a word of complaint. I'd always been given to believe that men expected women to do these sorts of things for them. It had never been an issue for me, growing up surrounded by servants, and maybe I should have offered to help. That was likely the polite thing to do, though I wasn't sure the usual manners applied when you were being held somewhere against your will.

After we finished eating, I prepared myself for my usual day locked up while Wicked went out to do gods knew what in the forest. I was so bored and weary of this. None of his books were any good, and I couldn't do anything while I was trapped in here and he took the only key with him. I examined every inch of my small prison, testing the hinges and the locks, but it may as well have been a stone fortress.

"Please don't leave me here alone again," I said. "I promise I'll be good. I just need to get out of here for a few hours." I put on my most pleading expression and even clasped my hands under my chin for good measure. "I'll make you dinner tonight. How about that?"

He arched a sardonic eyebrow. "Do you have any idea how to cook, *Princess*?"

I narrowed my eyes. What an ass. I had absolutely no idea how to cook, but how hard could it be? "Of course I can. What do you take me for?"

He gave me a look that suggested he knew I was lying and then strode over to where his boots sat against the wall.

"Fine," he said. "But if you try anything, then I'll make

you sleep outside, chained to the battlements tonight. It's supposed to snow later."

"I promise," I said sweetly, my voice dripping with honey while I batted my eyes. The look he threw me was filled with utter suspicion.

The sun was out today, the air warmer than it had been in days. I left my cloak behind, opting only for my heavy tunic and overcoat, and Wicked did the same.

We emerged to a bright blue sky stretching overhead, and I wondered if he was lying about the snow just to be a jerk.

"Come on," Wicked said. "You walk in front and don't get any ideas."

I tossed him a dirty look and did what he asked, marching ahead as we slunk into the forest. The only time he spoke was to direct me to where we were going. He probably could have made it in a quarter of the time without me slowing him down, but he didn't complain.

"We're almost there," he finally said as he brushed past me and we entered a clearing. In the center of it sat a large iron cage.

"What is that?" I asked, my hand drifting to my throat in horror.

Was he going to leave me out here in that?

He cast a look over his shoulder, and I didn't need words to tell me that was exactly what he'd planned.

Chapter Twelve

" I am not going in there," I declared. He didn't answer as he pulled a leather wrap out of his pack. He unrolled it onto the ground, revealing a set of iron tools with worn wooden handles.

"Sit down and be quiet," he said, pointing to a large rock nearby. "You said you wouldn't cause trouble if I brought you with me, and I'm holding you to that." He stared at me, not wavering, waiting for me to comply. "The temperature is supposed to drop tonight," he said, reminding me of his threat to leave me out on the battlements.

Without saying a word, I folded my arms, put my nose in the air and sank down on the rock where he pointed, pretending like this had been my idea all along. "Oooh, what a comfy rock," I said, wiggling my butt against it. "This is so much better than my *cage*."

As usual, he ignored me while he returned to what he was doing. He used the various tools—a screwdriver, a hammer, a wrench—to make adjustments to the cage, first working on the outside and then moving to the door. I stared at the sky and let out a long breath.

My elbows planted on my knees, I watched him work, enjoying the way his muscles shifted under his tunic. He'd taken off the heavier overcoat while he'd worked, the sun warm despite the thin crust of snow on the ground.

I let out another dramatic sigh, and he tossed me an impatient look. When he turned away, I grinned.

It was then I noticed he'd left his dagger lying on the ground next to him. He was working on the door to the cage, crouching on the balls of his feet, his body half in and half out. Should I do it? Now was as good a chance as any, and I'd been waiting for an opportunity like this. I'd have to move faster than I ever had in my life, but I hadn't seen an opening this good in weeks. Who knew when he'd let his guard down like this again?

I took a slow breath, trying to calm my heartbeat. I couldn't alert him to any change in my demeanor. He'd sense it—I was sure of it. I edged off the rock so I was hovering just above it, my hands braced for leverage. I'd only get one attempt to do this, and if I messed up, it was over. Counting down from three, I readied myself, and then I ran.

Crashing into Wicked, I knocked him over, sending him toppling into the cage. I slammed the door shut and flipped the lock before he launched himself at me with a snarl. I leaped back, but the bars and the door held fast as he shook it and roared. "Rowan! Open this right now." For a moment, I was too shocked to move. I couldn't believe that worked. And oh my gods, was he pissed.

I stepped forward to pick up the dagger that lay just

outside the cage, beyond his reach. He lunged again, the entire cage shifting, and I nearly fainted from how hard my heart was beating.

"Rowan, open this right now," he hissed. I held up the dagger with a shaking arm and shook my head. I needed to end this, but I couldn't get near enough to slit his throat. Even if I could, I wasn't sure if I could go through with it. It was one thing to tell yourself you're going to kill someone and quite another thing to actually do it.

"Rowan!" he roared again, hurling his body at the bars. I had to get out of here. Now.

"I'm sorry," I said, not sure what I was apologizing for and then turned and ran as fast as I could.

Once again on the run, I headed in the castle's direction, hoping I'd find my way as I got closer. Otherwise, I'd have to find somewhere to hide. If he caught me, I was finished. He was furious. I prayed the cage would hold him. Clearly he'd intended it for the Reaper, who didn't exactly sound like a kitten, so Wicked had to have made it pretty strong.

But strong enough to hold a seriously apoplectic Fae? Gods, I hoped so.

Running as fast as I could, I cast glances over my shoulder, terrified of seeing that familiar shape pursuing me. Would he catch me again? I pumped my arms and legs, dashing through the trees, a prayer on my lips.

Suddenly, I went flying, something wrapping around my legs. I crashed into the ground, a heavy weight landing on top of me. I kicked and screamed and thrashed, but he had me. A low growl came from his throat as he flipped me over and pressed me into the cold ground, seizing my wrists in his hands. Slamming them to the earth, I cried out as Wicked landed on top of me with all of his weight.

"Let me go!" I screamed, bucking and kicking. But he was solid and immoveable, and I was completely ineffective.

"Hold still," he snarled. "I'm going to..." He trailed off, apparently at a loss for words.

"What? You're going to what?! Leave me in the woods in a cage as bait for the Reaper and leave me to die?!" I screamed so loud my voice cracked.

"That's not what—" he said and I spit at him, saliva landing on his cheek and slowly sliding down. He growled and leaned over, bringing his face to mine, his big body pressing me into the cold ground. I writhed and fought and then suddenly stopped, my breath seizing.

Fuck. Wicked was as hard as a rock. I could feel his thick length where his hips pressed between my thighs, and heat rushed to my stomach. Our gazes met and his nose flared as I remembered what he'd said about his sense of smell. There was no doubt he could scent how wet I'd just become. Why was this so hot? I wanted to die right there of mortification.

For several long heartbeats, we stared at each other, our chests heaving, lightning sparking in the air between us. His dark expression was so intense, I thought it might melt me right into the forest floor.

A second later, he hauled himself up and pulled me to stand, clamping on to my wrist before he dragged me back through the forest. I'd never seen him this angry. It was obvious in the set of his shoulders and the way he ignored my protests while I stumbled to keep up.

Before long, we arrived back at the castle. He said nothing as he dragged me inside, shoved me into my cage and slammed the door. He didn't move, holding on to the bars as he stared at me, his chest still puffing in and out. My own breath was coming in tight, short gasps.

"I hate you! I want to go home! How can you do this to me?"

Suddenly, he swung open the door and stormed in, coming to a stop so close I had to press myself into the wall to avoid touching him. His hands planted themselves on either side of my head and he leaned in, his hard body and his hard cock pressing against me, caging me in. I squirmed, the space between my thighs tightening in response. What the hell was wrong with me?

"You can't be angry with me for trying to save myself," I hissed. He moved his face closer, his expression a mask of fury. I was sure I was about to die.

Forget the Reaper, Wicked would be the source of my eternal undoing.

"I'm not angry with *you*," he snarled and then he kissed me.

Chapter Thirteen

We met in a fevered rush, Wicked's mouth devouring me. His moan sparked through every one of my nerves as he crushed me to the wall, his hips thrusting into mine. There was no doubt he was ready for anything. His hands slid up the backs of my thighs before he lifted me up, my legs wrapping around his waist.

I drove my hips against the rigid length of his cock, seeking the relief of more friction. His tongue plunged into my mouth while his hands roamed along my ribs and skated up the sides of my breasts, his thumbs sweeping over their curves. While he kissed me harder, my hands slid into his thick hair. It was silky and luxurious, and he made a helpless sound in his throat when I scratched my nails along his scalp.

A moment later, he pulled me from the wall and, with his large hands gripping my ass, he carried me across the room and dropped me on the bed. He wasted no time collapsing on top of me, our mouths parting only for a breath before he kissed me again. It was frantic and wild, the sounds of our fevered groans filling the air.

I should probably put a stop to this.

But as his weight stretched over me, and he swirled his hips again, I was finding it hard to care about any future repercussions. There was only this moment, and *this* was a kiss I'd been waiting for. It was nothing like Ellis's kisses. It was like comparing a light breeze that tickled your skin to a hurricane that ripped through you and shattered your bones.

I wasn't entirely inexperienced—Ellis and I had succumbed to curiosity, hormones, and the security of knowing we'd be sharing our bed for the rest of our days, but that had been quiet and sweet and this was a chord wrenched from a taut string. This was raw animal energy.

"Rowan," Wicked said, his mouth dragging down my throat as he pressed hot, wet kisses over my collarbone. His warm palm slid under my tunic, skating across my stomach, his fingers curling into the waistband of my leggings.

My hands ran up his back, my fingers digging into the bunch and flex of all those miles of glorious muscle. I yanked on the fabric of his tunic, tugging it up. He pulled it off and then went for the hem of mine before I raised my arms so he could pull it up over my head.

After he tossed it away, he sat back on his knees, staring down at me with that hungry, predatory gleam that did strange things to my insides. It was a look that had once frightened me, but now it did things that scared me in entirely different ways. A second later, he dropped on top of me again, sucking on my bottom lip, his kiss deep and blazing.

"I want to touch you," he said, his voice ragged. "I haven't been able to stop thinking about making you come on my fingers." He pulled up, searching my face, asking for permission.

Grabbing his head, I pulled him down to my mouth. "Yes, gods, yes," I said. If he didn't follow through on that request, I might implode into an unrequited heap of tissue and organs. At that, his kiss grew even more hungry, his tongue thrusting into my mouth as if in mimicry of how he wanted to thrust another body part into me soon.

He squeezed my breast, kneading and pinching the tip, curving my back into an arch with a gasp. His mouth closed over my nipple as he flicked his tongue and sucked. Then he bit me hard enough to summon a cry that straddled the wobbling line between ecstasy and pain.

His fingers burned a trail down my stomach, his hand sliding between my legs and cupping me. I moved my hips against his palm, craving more pressure. With his other hand, he reached for the buttons on my leggings and flicked them open.

In recompense, I reached for his waistband, tugging on the laces like he was a gift to be unwrapped and appreciated for all its highlights. "Oh, gods. Wicked," I groaned as he slid his hand into my pants.

"Fuck, you're so wet, Princess," he said, his voice rumbling in appreciation. His finger slipped through my core, pressing my clit and sending my hips off the bed. I continued pulling open his laces and then wrapped the searing heat of his cock in my hand. His moan vibrated through me as I pumped my fist along his thick length.

We continued touching each other, his caresses driving me to the brink of madness. He slipped a thick finger inside of me, and I cried out as he thrust it in and out, adding a second finger and using his thumb to circle my most sensitive spot. I whimpered with helplessness, and he made an indistinct sound of satisfaction in his throat as he continued to pump and thrust, my hips swirling with the movement.

At the same time, I stroked him over and over, gripping him as his cock grew harder. His breath came out in shredded gasps.

"Tighter," he growled. "Tighter, Rowan." I did as he asked, and he moaned, his eyelids fluttering. "Fuck, yes. That's perfect." I gripped him hard, his hips also thrusting against me. We were a tangle of limbs, arms and hands and legs, hips gyrating and groans echoing into the quiet winter evening.

Our gazes bolted to each other, our cries grew more desperate and fevered. His dark eyes were a mix of emotions. Fury and longing. Vengeance and lust. I wanted to know every thought running through his head.

As he continued touching me, my release spiraled tighter and tighter. Sensing it, he moved faster, pressing down on my clit as I broke apart and screamed, exploding on his hand. His hips were pumping harder and faster in my fist, his movements becoming erratic. I felt him thicken and then he moaned before he released in a hot, thick spurt.

Both breathless, we lay next to each other, my hand still

around his cock and his fingers still inside me, our gazes locked as our heartbeats returned slowly to normal.

Eventually, I released my hold, and he did the same, pulling out his fingers and leaving me feeling strangely empty. His eyes didn't move from mine while he put them in his mouth and licked them clean.

The corner of my mouth hooked up with a mischievous smile. My mother would have had a fit if she knew what I'd just done. And with a rogue Fae, everyone called the Reaper, no less. Who *was* he?

Wicked rolled off the bed and found a cloth, cleaning himself up before coming over to wipe off my hand.

He then sat down on the edge of the bed, his head buried in his palms, and I scooted in next to him.

"So," I said. "That was..."

He looked up at me, his expression serious. "I shouldn't have done that."

I rolled my eyes. "In case you didn't notice, I was there, too."

"Fine. *We* shouldn't have done that."

I hated he was saying this, even if I knew he was probably right. "Because you plan to kill me?" I asked, sort of joking, but not really. "I knew that when I decided I was okay with doing this, so you know..."

He scowled as though I were the one to blame for everything and got up, storming over to the kitchen to make dinner. He said nothing while he worked, slamming the pots and pans and dishes. I kept my mouth shut as I lay on my stomach and admired the muscles in his back and arms, since he hadn't bothered to put his shirt back on.

Soon, the smells of food filled the air, and I slid over to sit at the table. Placing my elbows on the surface and my face in my hands, I continued watching him, just enjoying the view. Gods, he was beautiful.

He turned around to glower at me.

"Why are you so mad?" I asked.

"I'm not." He turned back to resume tending to the frying pan on the stove.

"Could've fooled me." His response was more silence as he finished cooking and then put the food on the table, dropping into the seat across from me. He picked up a piece of bread and tore into it furiously, his deep green eyes blazing, before he said, "Tomorrow, I'm taking you home."

Chapter Fourteen

"**W**hat?" I asked, my fork pausing in mid-air. "You are? Why?"

"Because," he said, sawing at his steak like it had personally wronged him.

"No. That isn't good enough." I held up my hand to count off his transgressions. "You dragged me out here. Stole me from my intended fiancé and my crown. Left me nearly to die in the forest. Then built me a fucking *cage* to use me as bait. You don't get to just decide I'm going home without telling me why. I deserve answers, and I'm not leaving until I get them."

His jaw ticked while he stared at me, his knife and fork gripped in his hands like he wanted to use them to crucify a bear.

"Is this because of what we just did?" I asked, wondering why he suddenly wanted to get rid of me. "Did you not... enjoy it?"

He let out a sound of frustration, dropping the utensils

with a clatter and pushing himself up from the table. "Of course I enjoyed it," he said, practically seething. "It was the most alive I've felt in centuries."

I frowned at that statement, noting the way his voice dropped at the end. Like he hadn't meant to say that out loud.

He walked over to the bed and found his tunic, pulling it over his head with furious movements. When he was done, he stalked back over to the kitchen and opened a cupboard, pulling out a glass decanter full of amber liquid. He poured himself a generous amount and tossed it back, finishing most of it in one gulp.

"If you're pouring that, I'll have some too," I said. With the glass in his hand, he studied me with such a conflicted sense of emotion, I felt like I was being picked apart stitch by stitch. He put his glass down and then found a second, dispensing a generous portion.

Our fingers brushed as he handed it to me, the sensation winding through my limbs and straight to my toes. After what we'd just done, this innocuous touch shouldn't have made the very marrow of my bones ache. But the way he looked at me left me feeling exposed and like I might tip off the edge of the earth.

With my eyes on him, I took a large gulp, and then immediately started coughing. The liquor burned straight down my throat, my eyes watering. "Good gods, that tastes like shit," I said, wiping the back of my lips with my sleeve.

Wicked was laughing, his mouth stretched into a glorious smile I hadn't seen before. It made his already gorgeous face so breathtaking, my heart nearly stopped.

"I'm glad you think this is so funny," I said, though I was laughing along with him.

He snorted and was trying to clamp down on his amusement, but I didn't want him to do that. His laugh was wild and big and seemed to filter out through every pore. In fact, some instinctual part of me wanted to make him smile that way forever.

"Do you want some wine instead, Princess?"

Still rubbing my tongue with my sleeve, I nodded. "Yes, that's more what I'm used to."

He grinned, and I savored this glimpse of a different version of him. One that was younger and carefree. I wondered what had turned him into this angry Fae living so alone in the woods. I didn't ask though, sure that would make him clam up and growl at me again.

He poured me a glass of ruby red wine, and I sipped it with a happy sigh. "That's better."

"Go sit by the fire," he said. "I'll finish cleaning up."

He began clearing the plates. "Do you want some help?"

He shook his head. "It's fine. Though next time you owe me dinner." Right. I forgot I'd promised to cook for him if he took me outside today. "I also recall saying that if you tried anything, I'd make you sleep outside on the battlements tonight."

I sipped my wine and looked out the window where the snow had started to fall in thick white flakes. The wind had picked up since this afternoon, the howl echoing through the empty castle.

"Um, about that... I'm sorry about that whole thing with the cage?" My voice pitched up at the end, because I wasn't actually sorry. "How did you get out of there, anyway?"

He cast a look over one of his broad shoulders. "You don't really think I designed it without a way to unlock it from the inside?"

"Well, actually I did think that, or I wouldn't have bothered shoving you in." He arched a skeptical brow. "Okay, yes. I still would have tried."

With a soft chuckle, he turned away and resumed washing the dishes.

When it seemed like the matter of both the dinner I'd promised and the threat he'd made had passed, I got up and moved to the worn sofa in front of the fireplace, my wine in my hand. As the wind picked up, I stared into the flames, feeling curiously comfortable and at peace with my surroundings.

Curling my legs under me, I set my head against the back of the sofa and listened to the crackle of the fire. Eventually, Wicked finished cleaning up and settled next to me, his drink full again. Ever careful about giving me space, he didn't sit too close despite the notable fact he'd had his fingers inside me an hour ago.

"Should we talk about what happened?" I finally asked, unable to stand the tension any longer. It hung in the room as if it were a nosy aunt fishing for the latest gossip. He looked at me, his dark eyes full of thought and his expression inscrutable.

"I wasn't going to put you in that cage," he said, surprising me and quite obviously changing the subject. "I was building it for the Reaper."

"I thought I was the bait?"

He huffed out a sound of frustration and ran a hand down his face. "You were," he said.

Past tense.

"And now?"

He pinned me with a dark look, but I didn't get the sense it was me he was angry with. I recalled the words he'd uttered before he'd kissed me. How he wasn't angry with *me*.

"And now, I realize I can't do this."

A band I'd been wearing around my chest loosened. I hadn't even understood how worried I'd been until that moment. In silence, I waited for him to continue.

He seemed to be hanging onto the edge of something and couldn't bear to look down. He took a deep sip of his drink, his gaze on the fire.

"I've been trapped in this forest for almost three hundred years," he said softly.

My brow furrowed as I watched him, studying his profile, the red and orange of the flames reflecting off the edge of his straight nose and the planes of his high cheekbones. He looked at me then, shadows of pain clouding his eyes.

"Why?"

"A witch cursed me to spend eternity within these trees. That's what these are." He gestured to the markings that covered his skin, and I had the strongest desire to touch them. I curled my hand into a fist as he continued. "To break the curse, I need an ogre's heart. She chose this spot near their nest to taunt me. They're notoriously hard to catch.

I've tried and tried for centuries and though I've come close so many times, I've never managed it. But they aren't immortal, and they've been slowly dying out and now there is only one left. If it dies, I'll be imprisoned here forever."

As he spoke, I felt the shattered pieces of heartbreak in his voice. His tale seemed to take on a life of its own as it wove through the room, wrapping around my arms and my legs and drawing me closer. Before I knew it, we were sitting together, my knees resting against his thigh, his arm casually thrown over them.

"Why did she curse you?"

He took in a deep breath. "We were lovers for a time. She ended up leaving me for my younger brother, who had his eye on the crown I was set to inherit. He was always more ruthless, and they were a better match. They colluded to get rid of me, the witch cursing me and banishing me to this place."

"That's terrible," I said, my heart squeezing as I imagined how that kind of betrayal must have left the caustic taint of venom in his veins.

"I've done some things I'm not proud of," he said. "You aren't the first girl I brought here, hoping to lure an ogre." Both our gazes drifted to the cage. "It never worked, though, and I let them all go. Eventually, I stopped trying to catch them that way."

"It didn't work? Ever?"

"No." He sipped his drink.

"Then why did you need me?"

"Not many wander to this place, but a few years ago, a wizard happened to pass by. He asked for shelter for the night, and I shared my tale. He told me only the blood of a princess would bait an ogre. That they wouldn't be able to resist its lure. It would put them in a trance, and it would be the only thing they could focus on. Then I could strike it down."

My mouth popped open as he gave me a wary look.

"It wasn't long after that I heard about the princess who would soon be of age and that I could win her in the Hunt. So instead of chasing ogres, I spent the last three years learning to bring down the biggest and fiercest stags in the forest."

He fell silent then, his arm still draped over my legs. I wasn't sure how to feel. Part of me understood how desperate he had become after all this time, but he had still planned to take *my* life for *his* happiness.

"I'm sorry," he said, reading my mind. "It was a selfish, terrible thing to do. After the last girl, I swore I'd never do that to anyone again. But then that wizard offered me what felt like a lifeline, and I was thinking only of myself. I had no idea you'd be so...well, you aren't what I expected."

"What did you expect?"

He shrugged. "I don't know exactly...I didn't expect to like you."

I snorted at that. "You like me?"

"You're a pain in the ass, Princess, but yeah, I do."

I tried not to feel good about his words, nor look too closely at why they made me feel that way.

He had still planned to bring me here to kill me. His story, while tragic, didn't absolve him of that. I backed away, moving his arm off my legs, not sure I wanted to be anywhere near him right now. The wind kicked up, rattling the panes. The snow was falling heavily now, white streaking across the window and blocking everything out.

"You took me from my family. You took me from the man I was supposed to marry. My friends and my home and my life, all so you could free yourself."

"I know," he said. "I promise I'll take you home tomorrow. I release you of any tie you have to me. You're free to go home and live the life you were supposed to."

I nodded slowly, not sure what to say. Not exactly sure how his words made me feel.

"Your brother?" I asked, the pieces clicking together. "He's the one responsible for the decree?"

Wicked nodded. "He's responsible for everything your kingdom has endured, Princess. For all the misery and control they hold over you."

"So if you had been their king..."

Wicked raked me over with a thoughtful look. "I can't pretend to know if I would have made a better ruler, but I wouldn't have done this." He swept out a hand as if to encompass some fractured dream he'd been clinging to for three hundred years.

"Why don't you look like the others?"

He shook his head, his gaze casting skyward. "They don't look like that, either. Those are glamors they wear to interact with humans to convince them to kneel. They think it makes them seem more godlike. More omnipotent."

I considered that, canting my head. "Well, it works."

Wicked huffed out a derisive note. "Indeed."

"I think I want to go to sleep now," I said, my hands pressed to my stomach.

"You take the bed," he said. "No chain, of course. Fuck, Rowan, I'm sorry. You have no idea how sorry."

"Yeah, okay." I stood to walk over to the bed and then stopped and turned back.

"Who lived in this castle?" I asked. "Why is it out here?"

"No one. I built it over the years, hoping one day people would fill its halls." Wicked paused, his eyes drifting over the room as if creating the life he'd envisioned but had run out of paint. "But when it was done, and I was still alone, I realized it was too depressing to live in it all by myself, so I closed it off and moved into this room where I've stayed ever since."

"You built the entire thing alone?"

He rolled his shoulders as though the memory was a painful one and met my gaze with one full of remorse and yearning. "I had nothing else to do, Rowan."

I nodded, digging up the seeds of my empathy for what it must have been like to be so lonely for so long. Climbing into the bed, I slid under the covers and fell asleep to the howling of the wind.

Chapter Fifteen

T he wind still whistled when I awoke the next morning. The fire roared in the hearth and snow whipped against the windowpanes. I sat up, shivering. The blankets had kept me warm, but the fire wasn't enough to stave off the chill in the room.

I looked around, frowning. Wicked was nowhere to be seen. I stood up and peered out of the window, only to be greeted by a wall of white. Where had he gone? Perhaps outside to use the latrine? I shuddered, trying to ignore my own pressing bladder. Traipsing out there had been miserable enough when the weather was mild. How I missed my palatial bathroom in the palace with its hot running water and its giant tub. I hadn't had a proper bath in weeks, having to settle for cleaning myself with a sponge and a bucket when Wicked went outside.

If he'd gone to see to his needs, then he'd be back soon. I didn't enjoy being here alone without him in this storm. I also didn't know if I could find my way to the outhouse without him in this snow.

Diving back under the covers to stay warm, I waited. I estimated when an hour had passed and then another. Where was he?

My stomach rumbled, and I decided the least I could do was fend for myself as I tried not to think about all manner of unpleasant possibilities. I was out here alone with minimal food and no real idea of how to make it back to the castle. For the first time in a while, I prayed that Ellis, or anyone, was out looking for me.

I walked to the kitchen and started opening the cupboards. I hadn't made him dinner last night, so I still owed him a meal. When he returned, I could have it waiting. I shivered again, grateful he hadn't followed through on his threat to make me sleep on the battlements. I probably would have suffocated under a mound of snow.

Eggs, flour, and sugar were here, so I thought I'd try my hand at making pancakes. I'd eaten them hundreds of times —how hard could it be?

I kept watching the door, hoping that at any moment it would open. Was I worried for him? Or for me? Maybe a little of both, if I was being honest. I set to work, finding a bowl and estimating the ingredients, mixing it all together, stirring and stirring, trying to smooth out the lumps. It wasn't perfect, but surely it was good enough.

Finding the frying pan and butter, I put them on the stove and spent several minutes figuring out how to light it. I wondered who had taught Wicked to do all these things— he was an excellent cook—or if he'd had to learn everything on his own. Finally, I got the stove working and watched in satisfaction as a yellow puddle formed in the bottom of the cast-iron pan.

When it seemed ready, I dropped in a dollop of batter and listened to it sizzle, rather proud of myself. With the spatula in my grip, I waited until it seemed ready and then flipped it and grimaced. The pancake was more charcoal than golden, and it wasn't fluffy. Maybe the next one would be better. I tried again, turning out another blackened disc that resembled cardboard more than food. I stared at the stove, wondering what I had done wrong.

It was at that moment the door crashed open and a monstrous frame filled the doorway. A leering skull covered in ice, a beast with fur and fangs dripping in icicles to the floor. I screamed and brandished my greasy spatula. "Get out!"

But the beast paid me no heed and lumbered inside, and then I recalled that skull. It had been weeks since I'd seen it, but now that I had my wits about me, I'd know it anywhere. Wicked shook the snow off his shoulders and pulled off the mask, his dark hair spilling around his shoulders.

"What are you doing?" He arched an eyebrow, stomping his boots on the floor and hanging the mask on the wall.

"I'm cooking. Where have you been?" He shucked off his cloak and shook it out. I winced. He was getting snow everywhere. It was going to leave a muddy mess on the floor.

"Miss me, Princess?"

"Not at all," I lied. "I was hoping the Reaper got you."

He snorted and then pulled off his gloves and overcoat

and finally his boots. His nostrils flared in awareness and at that moment I smelled it, too.

"No!" I yelled, pulling the pan off the burner where the pancake I'd been cooking was now burned to a crisp on one side and completely raw on the other. Wicked came to stand next to me, eyeing the stack of inedible pancakes I'd already ruined.

"I made breakfast," I said meekly. "Or I tried."

I waited for him to mock me. To scoff at what a useless little princess I was. Instead, he took the pan off the stove, stalked to the door and tossed the ruined food out in the snow.

"Hey!" I said. "I was going to eat that!"

"You were not," he said. "It looks like you forgot the baking powder. Can I help you?"

I opened my mouth and then closed it. He wasn't trying to make me feel bad. His offer was genuine. "Okay."

The corner of his mouth tipped up, and we got to work. He showed me what I'd missed and how to cook them. Before I knew it, we had a stack of fluffy golden pancakes ready to eat.

"Where were you?" I asked through a mouthful of food.

He blew out a breath. "I'm sorry. I promised I'd take you home today, so I was checking to see if there was a safe way to do that in this storm. But the pass through the hills is already blocked. I'll need to shovel it out when this stops."

"You went out in that for hours just to see if you could take me home? Now that the ogre doesn't want me and you have no use for me, you want to get rid of me as quickly as possible?" I wasn't entirely sure why his words hurt so much, but as my voice got louder and louder, I realized how much they'd cut.

"No," he said. "No, that's not it. I thought you'd want to go home."

"There was no reason to risk your life." The words came out angrier than I intended. He gave me an enigmatic look, saying nothing before he took another bite of his food.

"The ogre came that night," he finally said, so softly I wasn't sure if I'd heard at first.

"What?"

"It came. Closer than it's ever come. It did want you, Rowan. So no, this has nothing to do with you being no use to me. And I don't expect you to forgive me, but I truly am sorry for what I did." There was so much remorse in his voice I believed him. I wasn't sure I was ready to forgive him, though. "I just wanted to take you home like I promised."

When I thought of home, I tried to understand the hollow feeling in my chest. Did I want to go back? What was waiting for me there? A loveless marriage? A crown I wasn't that interested in? A life of being told constantly what to do?

But I couldn't stay out here. What kind of life would this be?

"How do you do it?" I asked finally.

"Do what?"

"Survive. Get supplies and food. You said you couldn't leave the forest. You left it that day you claimed me."

"I can travel short distances past the tree line. The day of the Hunt, I was close enough that it didn't bother me, but if I try to go much farther, it becomes painful. If I lose sight of the forest, the agony is so fierce, it's all I can do not to black out. When I was first banished, I tried so many times to leave, but it was no use. I couldn't make it.

"As for food and supplies, I have contacts in the village who I trade with. I hunt and bring them meat and they provide me with everything else I need."

While I listened, I understood just how alone he'd been all these years. The only people in his life had been out of necessity. I could hear the despondence in the fissures of his voice. It sounded like the echoes of a life barely lived.

"Why have I never heard of you? Surely someone would have noticed?"

"I wear the mask and let them believe I'm the Reaper. No one else knows there are actually two monsters living in this forest."

"You aren't a monster," I say, the words defiant.

He tilted his head, arching that soul-destroying eyebrow. "That's not what you said last night, Princess."

I scowled. "You can't hold that against me."

He grinned. "What are you smiling at?"

"I love it when you look at me like that, Princess. Like you want to strip off my skin and gnaw on my bones for dinner." He leaned forward, his voice dropping so low I felt a throb between my thighs and my cheeks flush.

"So you've been...alone all this time?"

"Mostly," he said, trying to make it sound casual, but there was a strain in it.

"What about...you know?"

He graced me with a smug look, his mouth twisting into

a wry smile that did things to me. "Are you asking if I've fucked anyone lately, Rowan?"

"I—no—yes," I stammered, my skin tightening, his words burrowing deep in my stomach. His grin was feral.

"You've got nothing to be jealous of, Princess. There has been the occasional visitor, but they've been far and few between. It's also been a very long time." His jaw flexed, heat burning in his gaze.

"I'm not jealous," I said. A lie.

"What about you?" he asked. "Did I sully your pristine princess perfection?"

I scoffed. "Don't flatter yourself." His grin stretched wider.

Why did I bring this up?

"How long?" I asked, apparently unable to stop myself from wandering this path.

His brows rose, and he studied me. I felt his look like a touch, a gentle, pressing finger caressing my skin. "I'm not really sure that's any of your business, Princess."

"Right, sorry. Of course."

He leaned forward, placing an elbow on the table and piercing me with those deep green eyes. "Not so long that I've forgotten how to make a woman come so hard she sees stars, Rowan."

Oh gods. He had totally done that.

My thighs flexed, and my nipples went tight. I swallowed the thickness in my throat, convincing myself not to ask him to prove it again.

His eyes dropped to my mouth and then lower as if he

could read the filthy thoughts in my head. Shit, he could probably smell it.

Thankfully, the wind saved me at that moment when it battered wildly against the windows, snow and ice drumming against the panes.

"I think this is going to last at least a few days," he said, frowning at the darkening sky outside. "I'll take you home as soon as it's safe."

I nodded and rubbed my arms, the shiver running over my skin having nothing to do with the chill.

Chapter Sixteen

As the wind howled and the snow fell, we cleaned up and then spent the next day awkwardly trying to give each other space and make polite conversation. I couldn't stop thinking about the way he'd kissed and touched me or the way he'd spoken to me last night.

As if sensing my thoughts, I turned to find him watching me with a penetrating look, like he was trying to see right into the center of my soul.

He tended the fire constantly, but the windows bled and the cold continued to seep in. We survived the day, and I wondered how we'd manage much longer like this. There was nothing else to do but cook, and eat, and stare at each other. I really tried not to think too much about what else we could be doing to pass the time.

It had only been a day, and I was unraveling like threadbare cloth.

After we endured another meal, I got the sense neither of us was hungry. It was just something to while away the time. As night fell, the temperature dropped, and Wicked kept stoking the fire, even braving the cold and snow to chop more wood. He refused to let me help, and I put up a feeble protest, content to let it lie when he shot me down. Soon the hearth was blazing, taking the edge off the chill.

"Is it always this cold in here?" I asked, blowing on my hands.

"It doesn't bother me," he said and then stalked toward the bed. He dragged the covers off and laid them in front of the fire. Next, he retrieved the pillows. "Sleep here tonight, so you're warmer."

With a nod, I slid off my chair and under the covers. I sighed in relief at the blast of heat that washed over me. "Where will you sleep?" I asked. We both looked at the stripped bed, and Wicked rubbed the back of his neck.

"I'll be fine over there," he said, uncertainty in his voice.

I rolled my eyes and lifted the covers. "Get in, you big oaf."

He headed toward me and stopped. "You sure?"

"We've slept next to each other for weeks. Why are you worried now?"

He seemed to weigh a list of options in his mind, and I wondered what he was thinking. Finally, he shook off whatever reservations were holding him back and approached.

After he settled down next to me, I had to stifle a groan. He was so warm, heat poured off him like a waterfall. I shifted, snuggling in next to him. I couldn't help it.

A heartbeat passed before his arm lifted and it wrapped around my waist, tucking me into the curve of his big body.

Now I had the fire at my front and the wall of his heat at my back.

"Mmm, this is perfect," I said, the breath of his low chuckle brushing my neck.

"If I'd known you were this easy to please, I would have done this sooner."

I gave his arm a playful smack, and he laughed. The sound was like the chiming of crystal, and I wished he'd do it again and again. I looked up, our gazes meeting.

"What are you thinking about?" I asked.

"Nothing," came his entirely too quick reply.

I narrowed my eyes. "Liar. Tell me."

He paused and then blew out a breath. "The same thing I've been thinking about for the past three days," he said, his voice dropping. "How wet you were. How you tasted on my fingers. How you moaned when you came."

My embarrassed laugh sputtered out. "Well, don't sugar-coat it, Wicked." He chuckled, the sound threatening to wrench me open.

"What are you thinking about, Princess?"

"Clearly about that now. Thanks," I said, and he laughed again, his hand sliding over my torso, his fingers spreading wide as my stomach swooped. "Confession?"

"Hmm?"

"I was already thinking about how good it felt when you touched me, too. About your..." I cleared my throat. "How it would feel to have more of you inside me."

The silence in the room grew so thick you could have sliced it and served it with butter. Wicked shifted closer, his body pressing against my back where I felt the evidence of how this conversation was affecting him. The heat between my thighs flared, and I heard his sharp intake of breath.

"If I take off your clothes, will you be too cold?" he asked, his baritone low and rough, his warm fingers sliding under my tunic, making gentle circles on my skin.

"Something tells me I'm about to get very hot," I said, my voice hoarse as he flattened his hand and ground his hips into my ass.

He kissed the curve of my throat and then dragged the lobe of my ear between his teeth. I flipped around to face him, barely settling before his mouth slanted over mine in a furious kiss that left us both panting. He pulled up the hem of my tunic, yanking it over my head and tossing it away.

My skin erupted into gooseflesh, partly from the cold, but mostly from him, while his hands slid up my arms and over my shoulders before he cupped my breasts and leaned in for another deep kiss that plunged straight into my wet, achy center.

"Rowan," he whispered, his mouth against mine. "I want to fuck that wicked little mouth and this pretty pussy and make you come with my name on your lips until I've completely ruined you."

"Oh gods," was the only response I could muster as he yanked off his own tunic and then tugged down on my waistband, pulling off my leggings and adding them to the pile of our gathering clothing.

"But what I really want is to taste you, Princess. I want to make you come apart with my tongue deep inside you." He rose over me and kissed me again as I slid my hands into his hair, pulling him closer, needing to feel him against me.

"Rowan?" he asked. "Tell me what you need. What you want."

"All of that," I said, breathless. "All that stuff you said. That sounds very good."

He chuckled, his eyes sparkling like shadowed emeralds. The sound was low and seductive, and his breath grazed over my now fevered skin. I definitely wasn't cold anymore.

Wicked placed more kisses down the length of my body, his mouth closing over a nipple before he sucked hard, causing me to gasp. He continued his journey, his tongue and his lips marking a path of our sins until his breath skated between my thighs. His hands pushed my legs apart, spreading me wide as he made a rumbling sound of approval.

He sat back on his knees and I lifted on my elbows and watched as he pulled off his own breeches, leaving him bare and beautiful and glorious. I studied the hard length of his cock, wondering how that was supposed to fit. He gave me a feral smile as he stroked himself with his hand while I watched in fascination.

He then crawled past me and lay on his back with his head against the sofa.

Taking my wrists, he pulled me over.

"Ride my face, Princess." He guided me over top of him until my knees were planted on either side of his head. He let out a sigh of contentment as he took in a deep inhale, his eyes closing.

Sliding his rough hands up the inside of my legs, I trembled as his thumbs swept through the wet folds of my body. He lifted his head, kissing the skin where his hands had just been, and then his tongue flicked between my legs and I let out a soft cry.

"Wicked," I breathed as he did it again, circling the tip of his tongue on my clit. My hands snaked into his hair as I sank down, bringing me closer, seeking the pleasure of more friction. More pressure. The stubble on his chin was rough and delicious as it rubbed me with the precision of a lightning bolt.

His hands gripped my waist as he guided me over his mouth, my hips moving back and forth like I was taming a stallion. He moaned, the coarse sound rattling through my bones and scorching my blood.

I moved faster and faster, grinding down against him as I gripped the edge of the sofa to keep my balance.

"That's it," he growled. "Ride me, little Princess. Come apart for me." I did as he asked, using him for my pleasure as his tongue thrust inside me and my clit stroked against his face, the sensation winding me up tighter and tighter. I cried out, tossing my head back, the tendrils of my hair tickling my back. This was the most intense pleasure I'd ever experienced.

Wicked made a sound that was part groan and part growl as I tore apart with a scream. He held on to my hips, dragging me across his mouth as I surged through my climax. One of my hands gripped in his hair, the other hung onto the sofa so tight my knuckles were white.

When the waves of the aftershock subsided, Wicked flipped me off him and sat with his back to the sofa. Pulling me over him, my hips straddled his. I grabbed his shoulders as I slid myself along the length of his hard heat that pressed between my thighs. He moaned, his eyes closing for a moment, his large hands clamping on my hips.

Gripping him with my hand, I lifted myself higher, fit the head to my entrance, and slowly eased myself down. "Fuck," he hissed. "Gods, you're so tight. You feel amazing." Still guiding my hips with his hands, he slid me higher and then thrust his hips, his cock spearing into me.

I gasped at the sensation. The ache and the stretch and gods, this was the most exquisite bliss. He did it again, the veins on his neck standing out as he seemed to be trying to clamp down on himself. But I didn't want him to restrain anything or hold back. I wanted everything.

"Let go," I whispered, pressing my forehead against his.

I dragged my nails down his chest and up his arms, skimming over his biceps and the swell of his shoulders. Gripping his face in my hands, I pressed my thumbs into his bottom lip as I rocked my hips, our cries growing frantic as he thrust into me over and over.

He bit the tip of my thumb, sucking it into his mouth while he ground me down hard against him. His head dipped where he took my nipple in his mouth, biting down as one hand squeezed the flesh of my ass and the other reached between my legs, where he stroked my clit.

Warm tension spread out over my body as we moved together, our moans and cries backdropped only by the crackle of the hearth. A moment later, I shattered again, crying out, my release washing over me in wave after wave. Wicked grunted low in his chest and then flipped me over, pushing me to the floor, one hand coming under my knee as he drove into me deeper. I hung on to his shoulders, his mouth crashing into mine, his tongue and his cock both thrusting into me with unleashed abandon.

He moved faster and faster, his movements becoming erratic, until he let out a moan that seemed to shake the ground as a shudder rippled over his body. "Rowan," he gasped. "Oh fuck, Princess." He stopped, his eyes shuttered for a moment as if he needed a second to gather himself. Then he lay on top of me, his warm skin silky with a sheen of sweat. I ran my hands over his back, savoring the hard planes of muscle as he slowed his movements.

When he'd recovered, he let out a low groan and kissed me deeply, his tongue sweeping into my mouth. He rolled off me, landing on the blankets and tucking me in next to him, one hand trailing up my side, and the other tracing the lines of my face as he stared at me.

"That was incredible," he said. "I haven't felt like that in so long."

"You're just saying that because it's been like a hundred years," I joked and he grinned.

"I assure you that isn't the case, Princess." He lowered his head and kissed me again, peering at me with sincerity. "I haven't felt like that ever."

Immediately, my hunger for him stirred, and I hitched my leg over his hips as he drew me in. He was hard again, and his chest rumbled in satisfaction as I gripped his cock in my hand.

"You mentioned something about my mouth earlier?" I asked innocently, blinking up at him with the beguiling expression of a disobedient angel. His smile hooked up at the corner, his eyes gleaming with delight.

"If you spoil me like this, I might reconsider bringing you home, after all."

I pushed him back and straddled his hips, leaning down to kiss his chest and then his stomach before I peered up at him with a wink.

"I guess that's a chance I'll just have to take."

Chapter Seventeen

We waited out the storm for several more days, the snow blowing fiercely. Wicked checked our food stores, his brow furrowing in worry. "If we can't get to the village soon, we'll have to start rationing," he said. He walked to the window and peered outside. "This can't last much longer."

"Hmm, mmm," I murmured from the bed, not really caring. We'd spent almost every waking moment of the past days reveling in the taste and touch and smells of each other. Wicked had me in every way I could think of and some I'd had no idea were possible. I was an entirely new woman, my muscles jelly and my legs liquid.

He looked at me with fondness, a small smile on his face. "How are you feeling, Princess?"

"Lonely," I said, pulling up the covers and gesturing him over. He grinned and took me up on my offer, snuggling in next to me.

It took another day before the wind finally died down.

Wicked went outside immediately and came back to report the worst of the storm was over. "I'm going to shovel the pass so we can get you home. I'll be back in a few hours." He didn't wait for me to respond as he slammed the door behind him without another glance.

I stared at the door, my heart thumping in my chest. Was he still so eager to get rid of me? I tried not to let it bother me. I didn't belong here. I was supposed to go home and live the life that had been planned for me. This had been a brief, if rather enjoyable interlude, even if it hadn't started out that way.

As promised, he returned a few hours later, his cheeks red from the cold and exertion of digging out the snow.

"It wasn't as high as I expected it to be," he said. "We can go today. Get dressed. I'll carry your things."

He started picking up my scattered clothing and stuffing them into the bag he'd retrieved for me all those weeks ago, not looking my way. Slowly, I followed suit as he traipsed about the room with purpose. He couldn't seem to move fast enough as he haphazardly stuffed everything in and then scanned the small area, looking for anything he might have missed.

I sat on the edge of the bed, feeling small and forgotten and used. His expression was dark and furious.

"Wicked," I said. "I could stay and—"

"No," he cut me off, his eyes flashing. "You can't stay here any longer. I should never have brought you out here. This was all a mistake."

"But what about...this?" I gestured between us to encompass all that we'd shared the past few days. He'd made me feel beautiful and wanted and cherished. He'd told me I was brave and clever and that I reminded him of what it felt like to be alive. Had it all been a lie?

"We were just passing the time, Rowan. It was nice, but it's time for you to go." Those words punched a raw gaping hole right through my chest, my stomach clenching.

"It was nice?" I asked, hearing the lock on yet another future I'd imagined clicking shut. "Nice?"

"Yes," he replied, his mask of indifference held in place.

"You said you'd never had it so good," I whispered. "You told me it was amazing." Rifts formed in my heart, the cracks spreading out as his expression remained stoic.

"It's time to go," was all he said as he headed for the door, grabbed my cloak and held it out to me. "You belong with your family. Not out here with the monsters."

I took the cloak and wrapped it over my shoulders, hating this. Hating that I'd let him nourish me like a parched desert plain and now, with one fell swoop, he'd swept a hand and washed it all away. I wasn't entirely sure what to name this feeling. All I knew was his cold indifference threatened to dissolve me into nothing.

Once I was dressed, we headed outside.

The world was covered in a blanket of sparkling white; the snow crunching beneath our feet as we headed for the pass and the doorway back to a life I thought I'd lost. One I was no longer sure I wanted.

We approached the narrow opening, the sky overhead grey and cloudless. The air was cold and damp, and I shivered the entire way, partly from the chill and partly from the pieces of my spirit crumbling away.

Wicked walked ahead of me, his steps full of purpose. We didn't speak and while we drew closer to the castle, my stomach tied into knots formed from threads pulling in a thousand directions. I wanted to see Margaret and my parents, and even Ellis. But this forest and its secrets had filtered into my veins and rooted me to the earth.

When we arrived at the gates of my home, there was a shout as the guards registered my presence. Ellis flew out of the castle, followed closely by Margaret and my mother and father.

"Rowan!" He wrapped his strong arms around me and swung me around. Placing me back on the ground, his hands went to my face as he peered at me. "Are you okay?" I nodded as my family enveloped me from every side, shielding me in the cocoon of their love.

"We've been searching for you for weeks," my father said. "There was no trace of you after that beast came back." He spat the words out like they were bitter orange peels.

"I haven't found a way to break the decree," Ellis said. "I've had the overseers working around the clock, but it's ironclad. I'm so sorry, Rowan."

"It's okay," I said quietly, my heart bearing the crushing weight of all my sorrows. "There's no need. He let me go."

"He did?" my mother asked, tears streaming down her cheeks. "Oh, thank the gods. You're home, and you can get married and Rowan, I'm so happy you're home." She wrapped me in a fierce embrace, as everyone collectively mistook the reason for my tears.

I pulled away to say goodbye to Wicked, but when I turned around, he was already gone.

Chapter Eighteen

"Come inside," my mother said as Ellis grabbed my bag where it lay on the ground, abandoned by Wicked. I felt just like that shapeless sack spilling out on the snow.

She tucked a strand of hair behind my ear and touched my cheek. "Did he hurt you? Did he—" she cut off, casting a side glance to Ellis and my father as if the question was too ghastly to ask in their delicate male presence.

"No. It wasn't like that. I'm fine. He didn't hurt me." At least not physically, I didn't add, the pit in my chest throbbing.

We went inside, the scents of the kitchens and the warmth of the lit hearths enveloping me in a familiar embrace. My mother held my hand the entire way up to my room, where a hot bath was being drawn.

I went through the motions, bathing, eating, and readying myself for bed. As the sun fell, I cast a look out my window, yearning for a small, shabby room in the heart of a broken-down castle.

Wicked would be cooking for me right now, something hearty and nourishing. When we were done, he'd pull me onto his lap and kiss me and touch me in a way that made my eyelashes flutter and my chest fill with light. When Ellis bid me good night and told me we'd resume preparations for the wedding, I feared no one would ever make me feel that way again.

"That sounds wonderful. I'm so happy," I said to him, our hands clasped as I swallowed the sour bite of the lies that tripped off my tongue.

For weeks, I moved about the castle like a ghost seeking its final resting place while preparations for the wedding drew into full swing. At night, I'd lie awake staring at the ceiling, my opulent bed the last place I wanted to sleep.

It was the night before I was to be wed when I slid out from the covers, pulled on my lush velvet robe, and sat by the window, peering into the shadows of the forest.

The moon was high; the snow reflecting a luminous glow against the sky.

A movement in the trees caught my attention. With my nose nearly pressed to the glass, I watched it. I knew that shape. The breadth of those shoulders and the cadence of those steps. My breath kicked up, striking me in the chest.

I didn't stop to think. I stuffed my feet into my boots and then pulled on my cloak and sprinted through the castle. A numbing blast of cold greeted me when I emerged into the night and headed for the spot where I'd seen him.

My breath fogged in the air as I ran, my boots thudding heavily with the pounding of my heart.

"Wicked! Where are you?" Gasps sawing through my chest, I searched the shadows. "I know you're out here." I directed a look back at the castle. Sentinels would be keeping watch over the grounds. If I remained in sight, wearing my nightgown, and shouting into the forest, someone would alert the king, eventually. "I saw you!"

I plunged deeper into the trees, the darkness closing around me like a fist. "Please. Wicked."

Finally, a form melted from the gloom, taking the shape of my desire. He wore his great fur cloak, his hair loose and blowing in the breeze. He was beautiful and brutal, and the sight of him sliced through every layer of feigned emotion I'd been building.

"Go back inside, Rowan." His voice bore the texture of smoke and secrets. He came closer, moonlight reflecting off his strong jaw and high cheekbones. His dark eyes flashed, his mouth set into a grim line. "That's where you belong."

"What are you doing out here?" I pulled my cloak tighter, my teeth chattering. My feet were bare inside my boots, and the cold seeped in from the earth.

"Nothing." His face was tense as his gaze darted to the sentries posted on the battlements. I rolled my eyes.

"You're obviously lying." I stepped closer, only inches separating us. My body drew closer to his like the sky pulling on the stars. "Tell me why you're here."

Wicked stepped back, putting distance between us. Refusing to let it hurt, I took a step closer. "What are you doing here?"

"Go back inside, Princess."

"Tell me why you threw me out. Why you wanted to be rid of me so quickly after everything we shared? That meant something to me. Did it mean nothing to you?" My voice cracked, pain bleeding out between the syllables.

His jaw clenched, his eyes blazing. "No. It meant nothing." I swallowed as the burn of his words traveled down my throat and squatted in my gut. "Go back inside, Princess."

"No," I said, sure I detected the same flavor of the lies I'd been telling myself for weeks. Sure he hadn't been faking everything he'd said and done. "I won't go back inside until you talk to me."

"Then I'm leaving," he said, turning his back and stalking into the forest.

"You're not getting away from me that easily!" He didn't stop, walking deeper and deeper into the woods as I trailed him like a persistent shadow. "Come back here!"

Finally, he stopped and whirled so quickly I crashed straight into his bulk and nearly toppled over. "Go back home," he snarled, his teeth gritted. But it wasn't fury in his eyes. It was panic and fear and an unmistakable tremor of longing.

"I'm not going anywhere until you talk to me!"

"Go home!" he roared. "Why do you insist on bothering me?"

His words were intended to be a slap, but I countered back, prodding at the tender places he refused to acknowledge.

"Because I love you, you asshole!" The declaration was a gauntlet thrown. One I hadn't even realized I'd been clutching. "I'm going to help you capture that ogre, and I'll carve out its heart myself." I stepped closer, my hands fisting into the thick collar of his cloak. "And if that beast dies before I can do that, then I'll stay in this forest with you forever. Do I make myself clear?"

Wicked's eyes darkened, his pupils flaring into dark black pits of nothing, and he let out a whoosh of air like I'd lifted up my foot and kicked him straight in the stomach. He seemed to bend in on himself as he folded, when a noise in the leaves summoned our attention.

A bulk moved toward us, shadowed by the darkness. It was huge—even taller than Wicked and built like a barrel with arms and legs. Dark green skin glistening in the moonlight, its back was hunched and its hands were the size of church bells. It didn't look like it could move very fast, but it was probably best not to underestimate it.

"Fuck," Wicked said, shoving me behind him as he drew his sword. "Run back to the Castle, Rowan. Now." He snarled at the ogre as it lumbered closer, its beady black eyes glittering.

I remembered what Wicked had told me. That the ogre would be mindless with want for my blood. Maybe we could use that to our advantage. "I'm going to draw it away from you, and you attack it from behind. It'll follow me. You said it wouldn't be able to resist."

He looked back at me, his expression thunderous. "No. Absolutely not."

"On the count of three," I said, gripping the back of his cloak, digging in my heels and preparing to run.

"Rowan, no!"

"Three...two..."

"I swear to the gods, I'm going to lock you back in my cage if you do this."

"One!" I bolted, the ogre's head swinging my way as I ran as fast as I could. I heard Wicked yelling after me but didn't look back as I wove through the dense trees, hearing the rustle and snapping of branches. After everything, I trusted him. I knew Wicked would do anything to protect me. And if he failed, then there was no point to this life without him.

I didn't need to see to know the ogre was right behind me. I could feel its hot, fetid breath on the back of my neck right before a hand snagged the back of my cloak, tearing it from my shoulders. When the clasp pinched the delicate skin on my throat, I cried out, but I didn't stop running.

My feet crunched in the snow, branches snagging on my nightgown, the icy air whipping through the fabric and tearing at my hair. "Wicked!" I screamed, sure he had to be close.

The ogre lunged, an arm banding around my waist before it lifted me in the air, and I belted out an ear-piercing scream. I kicked and flailed, trying to land a solid blow somewhere it might matter. But the ogre was steel and sinew, and it squeezed me so tight, I couldn't suck air into my lungs.

I struggled against its hold, my vision darkening when I heard a crunch, followed by a sickening squelch, and then the ogre's hold slackened before we both collapsed into a heap on the ground. I screamed and tried to get the monster off me, its weight crushing me to the earth.

A moment later, Wicked was at my side. With a heave, he lifted the body of the beast enough that I could slip out and back away. Wicked's sword stuck out of its back, like an offering to the sky.

"You killed it," I said, my eyes wide with wonder and fear.

Wicked's eyes floated shut, and he let out a sigh so long it sounded like he'd been keeping it bound for centuries. He seemed to be in shock as he moved, pulling out the sword and then flipping the ogre on to its back. Its eyes were dull, staring at the starry sky.

He pulled out his dagger and leaned over the beast before he paused, contemplating it.

"Do you want me to do it?" I asked, knowing he needed the heart. I didn't want to slice it out, but I had sworn I would just a few minutes earlier. He shook his head, and I tried not to show my relief as he dropped to a knee and executed the grisly task.

Pulling out a cloth from his cloak, he extracted the glistening heart from the ogre's chest and wrapped it up.

"Now what?"

"I need to eat it," he said, and I wrinkled my nose.

"Wow, your brother really hated you." Neither of us smiled at my failed attempt to lighten the mood as our gazes met.

"I need to get back to the castle."

"I'll come with you." I stalked back through the forest, finding my discarded cloak and wrapping it over my shoulders. He seemed like he wanted to argue, but I held up a hand. "I'm coming. Don't even bother trying to stop me."

He pressed his mouth together, grunting in response. "Get on my back and hold tight." He bent down so I could do as he asked and then, without another word, we raced into the night.

Chapter Nineteen

Before I knew it, the familiar sight of the castle loomed ahead, standing on its hill, lonely and forlorn. I remembered the first time I'd seen it, terrified that this was to be my new home. Never did I think I'd be happy to be returning some day.

Wicked flew up the switchback, through the courtyard, and slammed open the door to the small room. He set me down, tossed off his cloak and moved to the kitchen. The sight was so familiar and comforting; it fired an ache in my chest.

Well, familiar except for the fact he'd just dropped the heart of an ogre into a massive stockpot. He said nothing as he worked, boiling the organ and tossing in ingredients for some kind of stew. As I watched him quietly, I got the sense he needed a moment to collect himself.

After all these years, what did it feel like to finally arrive at this moment?

When he was done, he filled his bowl and set it on the

table, meeting my gaze with a resigned look. Facing down the bowl like it was the firing line at his execution, he sank into his chair and began eating. We said nothing as he swallowed the contents, one fateful bite at a time.

When he was done, he pushed it away and while he stared at the table, I stared at him.

"Did it work?" I asked, and he shook his head.

"I don't know. I don't feel any different."

"Should we go outside? Test the boundaries of the trees?" I asked, just as I noticed the markings on his face were moving. They swirled like a painter mixing them on his palette. "Your tattoos," I gasped. They morphed into a shapeless blot and then slowly dissolved, leaving nothing but a blank canvas of Wicked's smooth olive skin. "They're gone." I stood up and tugged open the collar of his tunic to find more unmarked flesh.

"They're gone," he echoed, his voice hollow, his eyes distant. I stepped away, wanting to give him space. He planted his elbows on the table and dropped his face in his hands, his shoulders shaking. I slid into the chair next to him, watching as he collapsed with the burden of the years.

"Wicked?" I placed a soft hand on his arm. "Tell me what you need."

He lowered his hands and turned to me, his knees encasing mine and his eyes lined with silver.

"Did you mean what you said out there? You would have stayed here with me? That you..." His voice was rough, dulled to a jagged edge of hope.

"Yes," I whispered. "Of course, I meant it." I leaned

closer, pressing my hands against his chest. "Don't push me away."

"I don't deserve this. I don't deserve you," he said as though it were an absolute chiseled into stone.

I shook my head. "That's not true."

"I took you away so I could use you as bait. You can't love me."

I let out a breath through my nose. "You did, but you were desperate. It was wrong and you shouldn't have done it, but I forgive you. I forgave you the night you told me why. I love you. I want to stay with you."

His hands gripped my elbows as though he could save himself from falling.

"I can't give you anything but this broken-down castle. You're a princess. You're the brightest light in the sky, Rowan. You deserve so much more."

I leaned in closer, our noses almost touching. "I don't care," I whispered. "I have everything I need if I have you."

He held so still it was like a spell had frozen him to ice, and if he moved, he'd shatter into a glittering pile at my feet.

"Gods, I love you too," he said a heartbeat later and then he pulled me onto his lap and crushed his mouth to mine so hard, our teeth clashed and our noses collided, and I moaned because this kiss was the sum total of all of our longing. This kiss blew all the rest away.

My legs straddled his hips. He pressed against me, our mouths melding into one. "I love you too," he moaned again into my mouth. "So fucking much. I never thought..." He trailed off as I sucked on his tongue, and his groan turned into a helpless whimper.

After we kissed for so long, our lips were swollen and our skin was damp with sweat, we pulled apart, our foreheads touching. "Are you sure about this?" he asked.

"Stop it," I said. "I've been miserable without you these past weeks. I knew it the moment I turned around, and you were gone."

He closed his eyes. "After all these years. After the loneliness and the disappointment and the loss, leaving you there was the hardest thing I've ever done."

I smiled at him, tracing his bottom lip with my thumb. "When did you know you loved me?" I asked.

He smirked. "When you shoved me inside that cage."

I barked out a laugh and smacked his shoulder. "Stop it. That's not true."

He smiled, letting out a low chuckle. "It's true. You were so feral and brave. I couldn't decide if I wanted to tear your clothes off and fuck you senseless or hang on to you and protect you forever."

I took in a deep breath, my heart squeezing, and flashed him a coy smile. "How about both?"

He grinned. "Both sounds good, Princess."

"I'm just Rowan now," I said, feeling the last piece of my old life fall away.

"Won't they try to stop you?" He gestured to the forest and my home beyond, where I was sure someone must have noted my absence by now.

"By the laws of Aetherus, technically, I still belong to you."

"You don't belong to me, Rowan. I want you to be mine, but I'm yours too."

I touched his face, loving the feel of his rough stubble against my fingers. "Thank you, but it might be the only way they let me go, so for now, let's pretend." I winked, and he gave me that crooked smile I'd grown to love in this dusty, forlorn castle.

"I can't help but think you're making a terrible mistake." There was such anguish in his expression, it broke my heart.

"I've never been more sure of anything," I said, and the tentative smile that crossed his face seemed to loosen whatever rein he'd been keeping on himself. He pulled me closer, grinding his hips into mine.

"In that case, Princess, I can't spend another minute without my cock buried inside you." He began pawing at my nightgown, his mouth crashing into mine as he lifted me up and stood me on the floor. A moment later, his tunic and my nightgown joined the rest of our clothing in a pile.

He backed me against the table, his hands skating over my thighs and my ass before he turned me around and circled the nape of my neck with his hand.

"I missed you so much," he said, kissing the shell of my ear, his other hand cupping my breast and then rolling my nipple with his fingers. "I missed this soft skin, and this perfect mouth and this beautiful hair." He wrapped the length of it around his hand and then bent me against the table, his fingers sliding through my wetness.

He moved behind me, tugging open his breeches, and then I felt the press of his cock against my entrance. I moaned as he thrust inside me without warning, dragging his length out and then back in until he was fully seated. I felt his shudder ripple right through me as he pulled out and thrust back in hard enough to make me gasp. Warmth spread through my limbs, my stomach tightening already.

I clung to the table, my fingers digging into the wood as my back arched. As he moved faster, I cried out. His hand gripped in my hair, he pounded in and out of me, his other hand sliding between my thighs. We moved as one, our breaths shredded and our gasps loud in the silent night. He leaned down, his mouth clamping onto the curve of my neck as he sucked my skin and then dragged his tongue up to my ear.

"Come for me, Princess," he growled as he surged into me, and I shattered with a cry. He continued thrusting, his chest tight to my back, and his arm wrapped around my waist. His hips continued driving as I rode out my climax, and then his body tensed before he came with a prolonged groan. We moved together for another few moments as we climbed back down the peak we'd both just mounted.

Still shaking, he scooped me up and carried me to the bed and then covered me. Before joining me, he lit the fire.

"I can't believe you're here," he said, touching my face and running his hand down my side. "I love you, Rowan."

"I love you too, Wicked," I said, kissing him and then pulling back. "Do I get to know your real name now?"

He shook his head, laughing. "That *is* my real name, Princess."

"Oh," I replied, biting my lip. "I'm sorry I made fun of it."

"We'll call it even for the whole using-you-as-bait-thing." He winked, and I snuggled into him, warm and safe and happy.

Chapter Twenty

It was the morning of my wedding when we returned to the castle. My nightgown ruined from the ogre's blood, I wore one of Wicked's tunics that hung to my knees, my bare feet stuffed into my boots. We made quite a sight as we traipsed into view, my hair a mess and our hands clasped.

"I'll stay out here," he said, tugging on my hand as he tried to let go. I held fast and pulled him forward.

"No, I want them to meet you. Properly."

The welcome we received was lukewarm as we arrived at the gates, my mother so pale she resembled the fresh layer of snow on the ground.

"Where have you been?" she asked, keeping her distance as she eyed Wicked warily.

"In the forest with him," I said, taking her hands in mine as we both looked at the rogue Fae who now held my heart. "And that's where I'm staying."

"What are you talking about?" my mother asked, and I

explained everything that had happened as best I could. No one was happy about my confession, but thanks to the decree, they had little choice in the matter. Technically, he had still won.

I convinced them to call off the wedding and to hold the Hunt again and this time make my sister the prize. It was a role that suited her better, and I'd always suspected she'd make a better match with Ellis.

I promised my mother I was still her daughter, but that my place in this life was over. I could tell she didn't understand as she continually eyed Wicked, who waited for me to gather my things. Maybe in time, they would come to see what I did.

As he stood in the corner, a dark smear of black in the luxury of the palace, I smiled. It only made him look more regal. A hint of the prince he'd once been, forged by the wildness of the forest like an untamed spirit who'd finally broken free of its chains.

We hadn't talked about what came next, but I would go with him anywhere he needed.

When I'd packed everything, Wicked picked up the over-stuffed bag and slung it over his shoulder.

"Rowan," Margaret said, throwing her arms around me. "Why are you doing this?"

I touched her cheek and smiled. "I can't pretend to understand how things ended up this way, but trust me when I say I'm happy." Ellis watched us both, his eyes flicking to my sister, and it was then I knew what I'd always suspected.

The circumstances of our birth had promised him to me,

but that had never been what either of us truly wanted. "Margaret," I said, holding her hands in mine. "I want you to be happy, too." I looked at Ellis and she followed my gaze before I whispered in her ear, "This works out for all of us, I think?"

As my sister and my oldest friend looked at each other, they realized what this meant.

"I'll miss you," she said.

"I'll see you soon." She nodded, and Ellis came to stand beside her. "I hope you've been practicing your hunting," I said to him, and he huffed out a small laugh, his eyes shifting to Wicked.

"I might need a few pointers," he said to the strange dark Fae who waited for me, his hands full of my clothing. I smiled at them both as Wicked's brows drew together, a crease forming between them. He dipped his head in acknowledgement, and then gave me a look that begged us to please leave now.

With one last round of goodbyes to my family, I followed him out of the castle and into the winter air. We traipsed into the trees, and Wicked stopped, spinning to face me.

"This is your last chance to change your mind." His shoulders tensed as though he was really expecting me to turn around and leave.

I stepped closer, pressing myself against him, and arched on to my tiptoes. "Where do you want to go first now that you're finally free? Find your brother and take back what should have been yours?"

The corner of his mouth ticked up as he looked out to the horizon and then back to me. "Maybe someday, but first

I want to experience more than this fraction of a life before I'm embroiled in a war I probably can't win. As long as you're with me."

I smiled at him. "Anywhere. Everywhere. Always."

Ready for more hot enemies to lovers, forced proximity vibes? Read Feral is the Beast, Book 2 in the Cursed Captors Series.

Receive the latest updates about new releases, ARCs, bonus content and more when you sign up for my newsletter at nishajtuli.com.

Also by Nisha

Artefacts of Ouranos
Trial of the Sun Queen
Rule of the Aurora King
Fate of the Sun King

Nightfire Quartet
Heart of Night and Fire
Dance of Stars and Ashes
Storm of Ink and Blood

Cursed Captors
Wicked is the Reaper
Feral is the Beast

To Wake a Kingdom

About Nisha

Nisha has always been obsessed with worlds she cannot see. From Florin to Prythian, give her a feisty heroine, a windswept castle, and true love's kiss, and she'll be lost in the pages forever. Bonus points for protagonists slaying dragons in kick-ass outfits.

When Nisha isn't writing, it's usually because one of her two kids needs something (she loves them anyway). After they're finally in bed, she'll usually be found with her e-reader or knitting sweaters and scarves, perfect for surviving a Canadian winter.

Follow for More:

Website: http://nishajtuli.com/
TikTok: https://www.tiktok.com/@nishajtwrites
Instagram: https://www.instagram.com/nishajtwrites/